HyperLinkz

Road Blog

BOOK 6 ROBERT ELMER

WATERBROOK
PRESS

ROAD BLOG
PUBLISHED BY WATERBROOK PRESS
2375 Telstar Drive, Suite 160
Colorado Springs, Colorado 80920
A division of Random House, Inc.

Unless noted in "The Hyperlinkz Guide to Safe Surfing," all Web-site names are fabrications of the author.

ISBN 1-57856-752-1

Published in association with the literary agency of Alive Communications, Inc., 7680 Goddard Street, Suite 200, Colorado Springs, CO 80920.

Library of Congress Cataloging-in-Publication Data
Elmer, Robert.
    Road blog / Robert Elmer.—1st ed.
        p. cm. (Hyperlinkz ; #6)
    Summary: A summer vacation for the Webster family turns into an Internet chase across lost Web sites and a showdown with rivals Mattie Blankenskrean and Mr. Z.
    ISBN 1-57856-752-1
    1. Internet—Fiction. 2. Christian life—Fiction. I. Title.
PZ7.E4794Ro 2005
Fic—dc22   2004025716

Printed in the United States of America
2005—First Edition

10 9 8 7 6 5 4 3 2 1

Contents

Introducing...Road Blog

Evelyne Webster: Hello. I have to admit this is a little odd for me, talking to Austin and Ashley's friends like this—I mean, directly, that is. As their parents we've never... Well, this is slightly awkward and... Goodness, Tom, why don't you start?

Tom Webster: All right. Fine. This isn't rocket science, Evy. All we do is type the words, and they show up on the screen. But we'd better get to the point quickly.

Evelyne: You tell them, then. You're doing fine.

Tom: All right. The point is, we're concerned about our kids. Well, maybe not as much about Ashley. She's involved in the Chiddix Junior High soccer team and gymnastics, even tumbles around the house. But Austin! That's another story.

Evelyne: Be fair, Tom. You don't have to bring up that mix-up at school with the vandalism. You know the principal discovered someone else did it.

Tom: I know. That's all behind us.

Evelyne: And you have to mention the good things about Austin too. Give people a balanced picture. He's a good boy.

Tom: Of course he's a good boy. But lately he always has his nose in a computer screen, and half the time I have no idea what he's doing. So his mother and I came up with a great idea for something to help us really bond as a family—an old-fashioned family vacation. A road trip to Lost Lake Resort up in Michigan, where my folks took me when I was little. Boy, did I have a fantastic time back then!

Evelyne: You were two years old.

Tom: Well, my dad took lots of pictures. Anyway, the point is that we want Ashley and Austin to experience a family vacation like I did when I was a kid. We figured we'd have a lot of quality time in the car playing "I Spy" and singing songs as we cruise up Highway 51 to Rockford, across into Wisconsin, and straight north to...

Evelyne: Maybe they don't want to hear all the directions, dear. I think they'll understand when you explain Lost Lake is in upper Michigan.

Tom: Right. So we're getting close to Michigan, and what happens? Austin isn't looking out the window at the scenery. He isn't talking to his sister or to us. He's working on some kind of "blob" thing on his laptop.

Evelyne: That's *blog*, Tom. He explained that to us, remember?

Tom: Sure, I remember. It's his Web log, which is just a fancy name for a diary. But the point is, he's been spending too much time on the couch, too much time sitting, not enough time out doing what kids his age should be doing—running and biking and stuff. You know, things we did when we were kids.

Evelyne: And you didn't watch TV when you were young? What about *Lassie* and *Rin Tin Tin* and the *Mickey Mouse Club*?

Tom: Okay, but I didn't take the TV with me on vacation. And I probably shouldn't have let Austin bring that laptop. It's only going to get lost or stolen. Although, come to think of it, maybe that wouldn't be such a bad thing.

Evelyne: Tom! You'd better not let him hear you say that.

Tom: Just kidding, okay? But seriously, this vacation is going to be all about togetherness. And I'm going to pry our son away from that computer if it's the last thing I do.

CHAPTER 1

The Search Is On

"I'm going to get him away from that computer if it's the last thing I do." Mattie Blankenskrean took another sip of her naturally sweetened avocado-apricot purée and leaned back in her office chair. Why had it been so hard to shut down a twelve-year-old boy and his sister?

Or maybe he was thirteen. It didn't matter. What mattered was that he had found ways to get inside the Web and threaten her work. By her count he'd been Inside—where he had no business being—thirteen times in the past month. Mostly to game sites and such. But goodness, it was dangerous for a child of his age to be doing such a thing! It could even affect his health, and she couldn't let *that* happen.

Besides, if the Normal Council on Civil Correctness was ever going to succeed in its goal, it needed to convince this child—and his sister, though she didn't travel online nearly as often now—how misguided he really was. Either that or just plain keep him and his sister off the Web. Good thing Raven was working for her.

Raven Zawistokowski, or Mr. Z, as the children in his classes liked to call him. The perfect man to help her erase myths, superstitions, and religious foolishness from the World Wide Web. Mattie got up to check on him. Sitting in another room of their small office, he never took his eyes from his over-size plasma monitor.

"You'd better come take a look at this," he told her, taking a sip from his mug as she walked over. "You're going to like it."

Did he notice that his coffee had turned bitter and cold, now hours after dinnertime? Probably not. She had never minded working late either. Big dreams call for big sacrifices.

"Look. Right there." He pointed to one of the three open windows on his computer screen. He could keep track of several Web sites at once, the way a circus juggler keeps a chair, a bat, and a bowling ball in the air at the same time. "A Web site about Paul of Tarsus, or Saul as he was first called."

The site looked familiar to her, but she listened as Z explained.

"See? This new program lets me make changes from right here in the office, without our having to actually visit sites the way you did before."

Mattie lifted her eyebrows. Visiting Web sites in person

was *her* thing, and the means of getting there, *her* invention. What was he saying?

"Nothing wrong with the way *you* did it, mind you." His smile put her at ease. "I'm sure we'll visit online again. But if you really want to keep up with someone, even stay one step ahead, this is the way to go. It's much quicker than physically stepping into the Web site to find them."

She looked more closely at the monitor. Z's program *did* look pretty advanced. A search window let you look for people by name, the kind of site they might be in, even what they looked like.

"And you think you can find him this way?" She was almost afraid to ask.

"Absolutely." He leaned back and crossed his arms. "I'll know the second Austin Webster or his sister steps inside the Web. And then—"

"And then…" She raised her finger in a warning. "You'll escort him—and anyone else—directly out, without hurting him."

"Of course." He smiled again. "I like kids. You know I'd never do anything to put them in danger. In fact, that's what we're all about here at NCCC, right? Protecting the public from itself?"

Mattie glanced up at that same saying on the wall plaque

she'd hung when she had opened the office three years ago. At that time it had just been her, a lonely crusader working behind the scenes to make the world a better place. Now, with a little help...

"And here—see?" Mr. Z pointed at two side-by-side windows on his jumbo screen. "Before is on the left. After is on the right."

She glanced at the site about religious superstition, one of her favorite subjects to fix. This site was *www.paulsjourneys.net.*

"On the left you see the legend of how this fellow Saul was on his way to Damascus when somehow God appeared to him, he was blinded, and he turned into an intolerant religious fanatic."

Mattie nodded. No doubt the Web site's owner would appreciate how Z was clearing up the story, adjusting it so it was more rational and not so offensive to those who, like her, weren't religious. After all, hurting people's feelings was bad enough, but saying people needed God, well... Who could have a problem with their changing things a bit?

"And then on the right, here's my new version, what we believe must have *really* happened. Saul's out in the heat too long, looks straight up at the sun by accident, gets really dizzy, and is temporarily blinded. End of story. Period. All sorts of legends grew out of that simple little accident.

"And see? I've even added a couple links to some cool sunglasses ads. Nice touch, eh?"

He moved the computer mouse so the pointer highlighted the first window, and then he hit Delete with a wave of his hand.

"All gone," he told her with a satisfied smirk. "Now anyone who checks out that site will learn what *really* must have happened. Without the silly religious myth."

"Good work." Mattie nodded and turned back to her desk. *Perfect, in fact.* But she still had one problem. Or, rather, two.

"You'll let me know when you locate the Websters, won't you?"

"I'm on it."

CHAPTER 2

Are We There Yet?

"Gently!" Austin's mom held her jawbone as they rumbled down yet another bumpy gravel trail, probably the one Lewis and Clark would have used if they had ever chosen to travel the woods of north-central Wisconsin. Which they hadn't, of course. "Do you think you could slow down, Tom?"

THUNK! Their poor, overloaded minivan bottomed out on yet another pothole, nearly sending Austin, Ashley, and Jessi through the roof.

"Good going, Dad!" Austin clapped his father on the shoulder. Anything to lighten everyone's mood. "I'll fix the tire."

"Tire's fine," Mr. Webster answered through clenched teeth. "Road's fine. Everything's fine."

So things were fine, if being lost in the woods for nearly an hour was what he meant by "fine." Austin's mom had long since given up trying to help with directions. She just held on for dear life as they barreled down the tiny back roads, no doubt going in circles.

"I think we've been this way before." Ashley pointed out a crooked tree in the headlights. "That looks familiar."

"No, it doesn't," snapped her father.

Whoops. Austin made a mental note to stay quiet.

"Maybe we should sing." That was Jessi's contribution, and when no one said anything, she started in on the first verse of "One Hundred Bottles of Pop on the Wall."

"Jessi," Ashley whispered to their aunt. "Not now."

Strange as it seemed to some people, Jessi really *was* Austin and Ashley's aunt—even though she was around their age and went to the same school. Fact was, she was their mom's way-little sister. Funny how things worked out sometimes.

"Aha!" Finally their dad became his chipper self again. "I think I see it up ahead."

"It" would be the Whispering Pines Family Campground, the halfway point on their pilgrimage to the past: the Lost Lake Resort in northern Michigan that their dad had been so excited about. Austin wondered if the place would still look anything like the old black-and-white photos he'd seen.

"I see something too." Their mom sounded hopeful as they approached. But no one said anything as they crunched to a stop next to the abandoned general store/gas station, with its boarded-up windows. Weeds grew up through the cracked concrete driveway.

" 'Turkey Creek Store.' " Ashley read the faded lettering painted above the door. " 'Gas, hunting licenses, sundries...' "

"Boy, I could sure use a sundry right now," Jessi piped up. "One with chocolate sauce and a cherry on top. It's been ages since dinner."

"Sundries, Jessi, not sundaes," Austin corrected her. "Like little things you buy at the corner store."

"Oh." Jessi still didn't look as if she knew the difference.

"Well, at least..."—Mrs. Webster's voice trailed off as she seemed to struggle to think of something nice to say—"at least there's a light on in the outdoor phone booth. That means there has to be civilization somewhere close by, don't you think?"

Austin wasn't so sure, but as the grownups puzzled over the road map once more, he had an idea. At least it would be worth a try. He rummaged in his equipment bag to find his old modem.

"What are you doing?" Ashley looked up from the Christy Miller book she was reading by flashlight.

"Just going to make a quick phone call," he told her as he stepped outside with his trusty laptop. Sure, it was kind of scratched up on the cover, but it still worked great.

Actually, this was going to be more than a phone call. The old modem fit right over the end of the phone receiver, and the

800 number Austin dialed brought up his Internet connection. From there it was only a few steps to the backward phone directory (plug in a phone number, get back an address) and then *www.MapAnywhere.com.* Once back in the car, Austin used his battery-operated printer to pump out a color map of Turkey Hill Road, which crossed Norseman Creek before finally heading back to the highway.

"Would this help, Dad?" Austin handed over his treasure as his parents looked up from their upside-down map.

"Where did you get this?" Mr. Webster held Austin's map up to the van's dome light and scratched his head.

Austin shrugged. "The Internet connection was just good enough. Looks like the campground is 15.2 miles away."

Their dad looked at Austin's map again and grinned for the first time in hours. Then he snapped off the inside light and put the van back into gear.

"We were going the right way the whole time," he said. "Probably would've been there already if we hadn't stopped."

"Right." Austin agreed as they made a U-turn and headed back the way they had come. "We're almost there."

"Aren't you glad I made you bring that computer of yours?" Mr. Webster asked over his shoulder as they left the Turkey Creek Store behind in a cloud of dust and gravel.

"Yeah, Dad." Austin grinned and then ducked when a hand came back to muss his hair.

"I still think a sundry sounds good," Jessi sighed, and they all laughed.

She's joking, right? Austin wasn't always sure.

And his mother had a friendly warning for him.

"Austin, your father and I want you to get out and exercise when we're at the lake. Do something active, something besides working on your computer. Promise?"

Austin raised his right hand in a boy-scout salute.

"Promise."

CHAPTER 3

Virtual Lewis and Clark

Pffft! Austin blew icy water from his mouth and shook his soaking head like a dog after a bath. But the big splash didn't stop him from paddling. Instead, he dug into the white frothy rapids even harder with his paddle, keeping time to the canoe leader's call.

"STROKE!" The man's shout was almost lost in the roar of the rapids and the hiss of water rushing over the boulders all around them. "PUT YOUR BACKS INTO IT!"

"I am, I am," Jessi groaned, paddling like crazy.

Austin thought the wooden paddles might snap like toothpicks from the strain. But the group did manage to keep their twelve-person dugout canoes from tipping over or spinning through the rapids. They shot through the river's natural water spigots like a watermelon seed between rocky fingers. *Pull right! Pull left! Watch out for that rock!*

"You think this is active enough to make Mom and Dad

happy?" Ashley huffed as she paddled her heart out like the men sitting beside them in the boat.

"Yeah, this is nothing like renting a paddle boat at the campground fishpond." Austin smiled. If their parents could see them now.

Or not.

For all their parents knew, Austin and Ashley—and Jessi—were getting a quick morning shower at the Whispering Pines Family Campground. Well, this *was* a quick morning shower, just not at the campground. Good thing Austin had wrapped his laptop in a plastic bag so it wouldn't get drenched. Still, he checked down at his feet just to be sure. No problem. But—

Sploosh! Another wave broke over the boat, and the man in the back looked their way.

"How you holding up, internauts?" He grinned from behind his dripping beard. "Is this what you were looking for at *Lewis&ClarkAdventures-dot-net*?"

"No complaints," Austin yelled back. "Our parents wanted us to get out and exercise, so..."

So if they couldn't ever meet up with real-life explorers Meriwether Lewis and William Clark, the Web versions were the next-best thing. One of the other crew members explained that they were on a swift-flowing section of the Columbia River in the Oregon country and that they could click on the map at the upper-right portion of the screen to see a detailed view of where they were.

And that would have been great if only they could have reached the upper-right portion of the screen. *Oh well.*

Austin saw that Ashley had started up a conversation with Sacajawea, the Shoshone woman who was in the middle of the boat holding her baby. But they were suddenly interrupted when the canoe shot into a full-blown, rough stretch of white-water. Like the gravel road the night before, this river had its own share of surprises.

"Whoa!" Austin did his best to hold on to his paddle as the canoe did a roller-coaster dip and spun out behind the back-wash of a major boulder. The front end of the boat tipped up, and the left side nearly slipped under the water. And that was it: One minute Austin was enjoying the scenery, and the next minute he was on his own—under water.

"Hey!" He gasped at the shock of the cold water and reached up toward the rolling surface. But the swift current wasn't letting up for a boy who'd fallen overboard.

Bam! Austin hit the next boulder downstream as he came up for air. Good thing he was pointed backward, so he sort of bounced off. With one hand still gripping his paddle, he poked his head up as high as he could and twirled around to face downstream.

Crack! The paddle split as he used it to fend off a rock.

Better to break the paddle than his leg, though. *What happened to the canoe, anyway?*

A moment later Austin shot to the top of a mountain of a wave, then down again and then up. The canoe popped up close by.

"Austin! Over here!" Ashley and Jessi both leaned over the side of the canoe and waved their arms. He waved back at them with the stump of his shattered paddle, but it seemed as if an ocean of wild river was still foaming between them. The girls might as well have been waving at him from another Web site.

Austin didn't know how much longer he was going to be able to keep bobbing up and down in the waves like this. Each time he hit another rock, he added another bruise to his legs, his knees, or his chest. The last hit nearly knocked the wind out of him.

He spit out another mouthful of cold water and wondered if he should try to steer for shore. But that might mean losing Ashley and Jessi and his ticket Outside to the campground. He hadn't forgotten that their ride home was wrapped in a plastic bag and wedged under the floorboard of the dugout canoe.

Of course, maybe he could e-mail himself back to the Whispering Pines office from this site—if he could find an e-mail link. But he'd rather use his laptop since it could take them straight home or from site to site, quick as can be.

The way things were looking, though, Austin might not have to worry about that much longer. Because just up ahead, a giant *swoosh* of a whirlpool had grabbed the boat...and now him. As quickly as he had been dumped overboard—*wham!*—he slammed into the side of the heavy wooden canoe—twice.

Ow! He remembered thinking he didn't like swimming around inside a washing machine, and then he felt strong hands on his shoulders, dragging him in over the side of the canoe. After that, everything got fuzzy.

CHAPTER 4

Time to Tell

"Pardon me, may I help you kids?" The woman looked in at them curiously, and Ashley poked Austin in the side. "I thought I heard water splashing in here."

Ashley watched her brother's eyelids flutter open, as if he were waking up from a nap. *Come on, Austin!*

"Water?" Ashley fussed with the twist-tie that held the laptop in its garbage bag. But despite the tie, she dumped a stream of water out with the laptop when she opened the bag. Austin was not going to be happy about this. "Uh, not in here. We just got back from…from sort of a shower, though. Maybe you heard the shower."

"Showers are closed for cleaning." The woman scratched her head and looked around the rec room at the three old kung-fu video-game machines, the telephone, the big trout mounted on the wall, and the Foosball table.

"Oh well, we'll be back, then." Ashley pulled Austin up with her as she rose to her feet. She tossed the dripping plastic bag in a trash can, tucked the laptop under her arm, and started for the door. Jessi had to be right behind them.

"Where's Lewis and—?" Austin's head was obviously still clearing, and Ashley didn't wait for him to finish his question. Instead, she dragged him outside before the campground hostess could ask them any more questions.

Speaking of questions, she wanted Austin to explain something to her: Used to be, they would come back from the Internet looking just the way they had when they'd gone in, no matter what they ran into while they were online. Lately, though, things had changed. Now if they got wet on the Web, well... She shook more of the river water out of her ear and buffed her hair with a damp towel.

And how had the campground lady heard the sound of the river? What was going on here?

"Did you get us out of there, Ash?" Austin asked, taking back his computer. Finally, he seemed to realize where he was. "Since when did you know how to do that?"

By now he was hobbling on his own through the campground—he would have monster black-and-blue marks on both of his knees pretty soon. Too bad he was wearing cargo shorts that showed his knees. The collar of his favorite Chicago

Cubs T-shirt had been ripped in the back, probably when he had been hauled out of the water. And his tennis shoes squeaked from being wet.

"Well, I'm not *that* dense." Ashley shrugged as if she did that sort of thing every day.

"No, I didn't mean that. You did good. I was just wondering."

Ashley wasn't honestly sure she could explain what she'd done, except that she had pressed a few keys on his laptop, followed some directions on the screen, and here they were. Only...

Only what had happened to Jessi?

"Uh-oh." Ashley stopped in her tracks and looked around. Maybe she hadn't pressed all the right keys. "She's still not here."

"You mean Jessi?" Austin looked back at the rec center too—a rustic A-frame cabin set next to the camp store, the swimming pool, and the shower house. He was probably thinking the same thing Ashley was. And that was...

"I think we're going to have to go back to the river."

Ashley groaned as they stopped in front of a large RV. She heard a crunch of footsteps on the gravel ahead of them.

"*There* you are!" Their dad spotted them as he came around the corner of the RV. "I've been looking everywhere for you. Your mom's been waiting breakfast for the past ten minutes."

"Sorry." Austin looked kind of like a sick fish, and their dad seemed to pick up on that right away.

"What in the world happened to you?" He came closer and studied Austin's face. At least he couldn't see the rip in the T-shirt. "Are you okay?"

"Oh yeah." Austin brightened up. "We've just been out—"

"We were out getting some exercise." Ashley interrupted her brother and gave him a quick warning look.

But their father crossed his arms and wrinkled his nose.

"What'd you do, run through a fire hose?"

"Oh, that." Ashley wondered how to explain.

"I mean, I told you kids to get out, but you don't need to overdo it, you know. And what's with your computer?"

"Yeah, maybe we were overdoing it just a little." Austin started to limp back toward their tent trailer that was set up in the next row of campers, past the bigger RVs. Ashley noticed that he didn't answer the computer question.

"And where's Jessi?" their dad asked. "Have you two seen her?"

"Uh…" That's about the time Ashley wished she could toss her brother's laptop into the Dumpster, forget the whole Web travel thing. After they rescued Jessi, of course.

A long couple of seconds went by, and Ashley looked over at Austin, who gave her a nod. Yeah, he seemed to be thinking the same thing, though maybe not the part about tossing his laptop into the Dumpster.

It was time.

"I checked around the shower house," Mr. Webster went on. "It's closed for cleaning."

Ashley took a deep breath.

"She's not in the shower house, Dad."

"I know that. That's what I'm telling you."

"Yeah, but there's something we need to tell you—and Mom. And I know you're never going to believe us."

CHAPTER 5

Confession

Austin's eggs were growing cold as he pushed them with his fork from one side of the aluminum camping plate to the other.

"I know we should have told you a long time ago." He tried to add to Ashley's confession, but he wasn't sure it was helping. "Honest, we thought about it bunches of times."

"Yeah." Ashley pumped her head up and down in agreement. "Austin even tried to tell you once, Mom. Remember?"

"You mean after that talent show?" Their mom poured another steaming mug of coffee for their dad. "I thought that was part of the stunt you two pulled."

"It wasn't a stunt, Mom." Austin closed his eyes. Should they start over? "It really happened."

"Oh boy." Their dad chuckled. "This is the best campfire story yet. But maybe you should save it for tonight, when we're roasting marshmallows."

"And I wish you kids would tell us where Jessi is." Mrs. Webster crossed her arms and looked off in the direction of the rec center. "It's not like her to go somewhere without telling us. Tom, do you think we should—"

He put up his hand.

"All right, then, kids. Straight up this time, without the campfire story."

"That's just it, Dad." Austin got up from the picnic table next to their tent trailer. "It was straight up the first time."

"Okay." Their dad wore an amused grin. "You take a picture of someone with your digital camera there, and it downloads that person onto the Internet."

"Right." Austin nodded.

"And then that person's actually there, on the Web."

"Uh-huh."

"Not just playing some computer game, but actually there."

"That's right, Dad. I know it sounds weird."

"Oh, not at all." Still the grin. "Actually, it sounds kind of fun, now that I think about it. Haven't you always wondered what it would be like to climb around inside the Web, Evy?"

"Tom…"

"No, really. In fact, I think we should *all* go there. Why don't we take a picture of the four of us, and we'll do some exploring, the way you say."

Austin looked at his sister for a better idea. How else could they prove their story to their parents?

Ashley shrugged, but their dad wasn't finished.

"And that's the only way we'll be able to find your Aunt Jessica. Is that what you're saying? By actually going to the Web site where she was last?"

"Maybe not the *only* way," explained Austin. "But it's probably the best way. Otherwise she might e-mail herself back to... Well, she's supposed to come back here."

"*Supposed* to," Ashley echoed.

"But knowing her, I think she might step on another link and end up anywhere."

Mr. Webster shook his head. "And here I thought you kids were ruining your imaginations with those computers. I guess I owe you both an apology. This is really rich."

Austin knew he couldn't say anything more. It was time, as his English teacher Mrs. Sanders always said during creative writing period, to "show, don't tell."

And, boy, did he know how to show! He was balancing his camera on a water-spigot post when a guy came walking by with his poodle.

"Hey, you want me to take a picture of you folks?" the man offered.

The poodle dragged on ahead, but the guy yanked back on the leash.

"Hold on, Roscoe."

"You don't mind?" Their dad came over to pose for the picture, and Austin handed the camera to the man, showing him which button to push.

"Be sure not to cut off our legs or our heads," Austin told him. "Everything has to be inside that little box in the middle."

"Austin..." His mom warned him not to be rude.

A few seconds later they all said their cheeses, thanked the man, and watched Roscoe drag him off down the lane.

"So!" Mr. Webster poked at his arm from wrist to elbow. "Now we're digital, the way you said?"

"Not yet." Austin shook his head. "I have to download the image onto my laptop first, and then I have to connect it to the Internet."

"And then?"

"Are you sure you want us to show you this way?" Ashley must have been having second thoughts.

"If it's the only way to get your aunt back." Their dad obviously still thought it was all a big spoof. And, of course, it didn't help to have Jessi show up just then, jogging up the lane, out of breath.

"You're just in time!" Mr. Webster was playing it now for all he was worth. "Austin was just about to download us onto the Internet so we could rescue you."

Jessi's face went white, and her eyes widened as she looked first at Austin, then at Ashley, then at Mr. and Mrs. Webster.

"But it looks like you saved us the trouble, Miss Jessi!" Austin's dad was still in weird mode. "I tell you what. Wait until tonight, when we're all settled at Lost Lake Resort. They have a nice, big campfire there every night. And I promise, I'm going to tell a Paul Bunyan story that's going to top even this one."

He pumped Austin's hand first and then Ashley's.

"But I have to tell you, that was one of the best tall tales I've heard in a long time. Good job, you guys. I'm inspired. And now that our morning walker is back, let's finish up breakfast, get cleaned up, and hit the road. Lost Lake Resort calls!"

CHAPTER 6

Keep on Blogging

"I keep telling you, Austin. I didn't do anything." Jessi rolled up her sleeping bag as she tried to explain for the third time. "I didn't touch anything, and I didn't mess with anything."

Austin's mind turned circles, trying to figure out the glitch. *Something* had made the programming do what it did. There *had* to be a reason.

"All I can tell you is I left the Lewis and Clark site the same time you guys did." Jessi didn't seem to be kidding. "But when I got back to the rec building, you were already gone. Nobody was there but a lady who came and asked me what I was doing there by myself."

"What did you tell her?" Ashley asked.

"What *could* I say?" Jessi shrugged. "I told her I was looking for you two. Which I was. She said you'd already been there forty-five minutes before."

"Hmm." Austin helped button up his corner of the tent

trailer so the roof folded down flat and the poles neatly collapsed underneath it. "So you got here forty-five minutes after we did, and we got here all wet from the river, and you—"

"Wet?" Jessi pulled at her sleeve. "Not me. I came back as dry as when I left."

"Weird." Ashley tossed a bucket into the middle of the trailer, ready for the next leg of their trip. "Seems like things online are all mixed up lately."

Things were mixed up, all right. Just like their dad's directions to Lost Lake about three hours after they hit the road.

Hey, bloggers, another road adventure with Austin Webster, lost somewhere in...

Austin looked up from his keyboard long enough to ask, "Where do you think we are, Mom?"

His mother started to say something, seemed to decide against it, and smiled back at him from the front seat.

"We are taking the scenic route somewhere in northern Michigan."

...h-i-g-a-n. Austin typed and then went on to describe what it was like to be lost for the second time in two days. The name of the resort was perfect, considering what they had

gone through to find it. Though since they hadn't found it yet, maybe the place didn't actually exist.

He stopped to look sideways at Jessi.

"I can't write with somebody looking over my shoulder." He tried to say it in a nice way, but it was true. Bloggers can't blog that way.

"Sorry." She leaned back to stare out the window. "I was just curious about what you were doing."

Austin quickly returned to his story about the nice scenery in that part of Michigan and the lake his family might never find. He also wrote that the battery in his laptop wasn't working right since it had gotten wet, wondering if anybody online knew how to fix that sort of thing, or if he just had to buy another one. *Right now I have to run my laptop off the car's battery, and that's fine, but—*

"You're not online out here in the woods, are you?"

The question almost didn't register at first.

"What? Oh... Uh-uh." Austin shook his head. "There aren't even any cell-phone signals out here. But..."

But the best thing about Lost Lake Resort, he wrote, *is something my dad never dreamed of when he visited as a kid. See, their Web site says they actually have a wireless network, which is pretty amazing if they do, but maybe that's what it takes to get campers these days. If it's really true, I'll be able to log on from our campsite, as long as we're close enough to the main antenna. Fan—*

"…TAS-tic!" Mr. Webster was waving his paper map and pointing and trying to drive all at the same time. "Didn't I tell you I could find the way here blindfolded in a snowstorm?"

Austin looked up just in time to see the carved wooden sign telling them Lost Lake Resort was just one mile ahead. Camping cabins, boat rentals, bait, swimming…

"Now, Austin." His mom turned around while their dad navigated them down a narrow gravel road, tree branches scraping at their minivan from both sides. "Don't forget what we said about getting out."

Austin reached down into his beach bag, pulled out a plastic diving mask, and slipped it over his nose and eyes.

"Just lead me to the lake," he snorted. "I'm an outdoor activity machine."

Well, that had the right effect. His mom laughed and his dad started pointing out things he thought he remembered from when he was little. As in "Look! There's the tire swing I fell off of and broke my arm!" and "Tamarack Cabin! I think that's the one we stayed in!" The lake shimmered bright blue just beyond the main grassy area; the place actually did look pretty cool.

But first things first. Before they got too serious about doing outdoor stuff, Austin thought he would test out the camp's network by downloading his latest travel blog to *www .Austin-Webster.com*. He located a signal quickly, which was good, and logged into the back door of his Web site, which was even better. Then all he had to do was hit the Download All Files button, and—*bam!*—the blog would be posted on his site for everyone to read.

Only problem was, Austin had forgotten about the photo the guy with the poodle had snapped of them…the one he'd already loaded onto the computer. And that, as it turned out, was a major problem.

www.Austin-Webster.com

"Look at it this way, Mom." Austin knew there had to be a good side to what had just happened to them. "We should be glad the van was parked and turned off before we came here."

"That's right." Ashley jumped in. "Otherwise it would have just kept rolling right down that lawn and into Lost Lake."

Still their parents didn't move. Were they even breathing?

"And that's not the only good news," added Ashley. "Because even though coming here was an accident, I think now you probably believe us. It *was* an accident, wasn't it, Austin?"

"Oh yeah." He nodded as he tried to figure out exactly where they had turned up. "Totally."

Finally his mother and father loosened up enough to start looking around.

"Don't anybody move," whispered Mr. Webster. He reached out and touched his wife's shoulder. "Are you there, Evelyne?"

"Uh-huh." Her eyes were as wide as his. "I see it, but I don't believe it."

"Me neither. Austin? Ashley?"

"It's all right, Dad." Austin tried to sound casual. "It's just a Web site."

"A Web site." Their father swiveled around for a better view. "Looks more like we're standing below a huge statue."

They were doing just that. And things were beginning to look familiar to Austin now. Above their heads towered a massive bronze statue of Abraham Lincoln sitting on a park bench with a stovepipe hat perched on his head. Behind that towered a huge, old sandstone building, taller than it should have been.

By now Austin was pretty sure. "This is my Web site."

"I can't believe it." His dad shook his head.

"Remember we were trying to explain all this to you?" Ashley stayed close to her parents.

"Yeah," said Austin. "Well, now we're on the Web—and on my site. This is where I post stuff. Pictures. Links to Christian bands. School projects. That kind of thing."

"Blogs, too?" their dad asked.

Austin stopped and looked at him. "You know about blogs?"

Mr. Webster nodded as he led the way around the sculpture. Being the tallest in the family, he stood almost as high as

Mr. Lincoln's boot, which didn't seem very tall at all. Now they knew what it was like to be Applet's size. Applet was Jessi's beagle, and that reminded Austin of something.

"Jessi didn't make it," he whispered to his sister. Of course, Jessi hadn't been in the photo the guy had snapped of them. Jessi would still be sitting back in the van, wondering when they would return.

"Pretty cool, huh?" Austin started to say, trying to lighten things up a bit. "You can go just about anywhere on the Web."

Their mother gasped. "Tell me you kids haven't been in here before. Er…wherever *here* is."

"It's really not a problem, Mom." Austin rapped on Lincoln's ankle to make sure it was solid. *Ouch.* "We've always been really careful. And my site is really lame. Nothing moves around in here, like characters and stuff."

"Wait a minute." That seemed to be too much for their dad. "You mean to tell me you can run into *live* things here on the Web? Things that move?"

"Sure—digital things." Austin put as much "old pro" into his voice as he could. "But here we're inside a picture of Bloomington, see? Notice the history museum?" That would be Bloomington, Illinois, the city next to Normal. "Last month I took a few photos of the Lincoln statue and posted them on my site, just to show what Normal and Bloomington look like. That's where we've ended up."

"And we're stuck here?" Their mother still had a worried look frozen on her face.

"We're not stuck," Ashley said. "We can get back a few ways. Sometimes we set up the laptop to make a direct-connect pathway back."

"Let's try it." Mr. Webster was shaking. "We need to get back right away."

"Uh, that won't work this time because I have the computer *with* me." Austin held up his laptop. "But another thing we can do sometimes is e-mail ourselves back using the laptop."

"That's good," their mom quickly said. "Do that."

"But that won't work either," Austin explained. "First of all, we don't know the e-mail address at Lost Lake. And second of all, the laptop's battery is dead."

By now they had walked all the way around the Lincoln statue. So what was left?

"The only other thing we can do," Ashley said, "is use the Web site's e-mail. You know how a site has a place where you can e-mail whoever runs it? Something like 'Contact Us'? We can—"

"Let's stop talking about it and just do it," their dad interrupted.

Austin studied his feet. This was not going to be good news for their parents, either.

"Well, that would normally be a pretty good idea, but when you do that, it sends you back to the Web-site owner's computer."

"And?" Mr. Webster didn't quite get it.

"I own this Web site." Austin held up his laptop. "And this is my computer."

He wasn't telling them something they didn't already know. But as his point sunk in, Ashley groaned.

"But"—he held up his hand—"I do have a pretty good search engine on this site."

Austin led the way to a door-size keyboard behind the Lincoln statue. Above it a small window appeared where the letters would pop up. "All we have to do is type in a keyword like 'Lost Lake' or something like that, and it'll take us there. Then we can e-mail ourselves somewhere from that site."

"Then that's what we'll do." Now their dad sounded the way he had back in the minivan, back when they'd been lost in the Wisconsin woods and he was sure he knew where they were going.

Charge on!

CHAPTER 8

Web Kittens

"You should have looked at the map, Tom." Ashley's mom didn't sound too happy about the way they were lurching through the Internet—sort of like someone learning to drive a stick-shift car. Whoa! Fasten your seat belts, please!

"You mean there's a map for this kind of stuff?" asked Mr. Webster.

Ashley could have told her dad there wasn't, but that wouldn't have stopped them from tumbling through the edges of the *Lost in Space* and *Lost Boys* sites (keyword: lost). Finally they rolled to a stop in a knee-deep sea of kittens.

As far as they could see were thousands and thousands of kittens, as if the whole world was filled with them. Black-and-white tabbies. Yellow tiger striped. Siamese. Longhaired. Short-haired. Jet black. Pearl white. You name it.

And the noise? Like babies who had woken each other up, most of the poor things were howling, screeching, and generally making a terrible racket. But Ashley couldn't blame the soft balls of fur. Anybody would howl and screech if four big, strange people suddenly dropped in.

At first the kittens had scattered, but it took only a second for them to regroup. One, a cuddly brown and yellow calico with green eyes, started to climb up Ashley's right leg.

"Hey, you." She pulled it off and held it out in front of her. "You look hungry."

The little kitten mewed in Ashley's face. Maybe it was.

"So is anyone going to tell me where we are?" Mr. Webster tiptoed through the kittens to where Austin was standing. Austin pointed up at a long white box floating about twenty feet above their heads.

"It says we're at *www-dot-LostKitty-dot-com*," Austin told them, squinting.

"And how did we end up here?" their dad asked.

Well, Ashley thought that shouldn't be too hard to explain. They'd tried to link to *Lost Lake Resort* from Austin's site, but Dad had hit the Return button too soon. Now they were just plain lost.

"Brother." Their dad rubbed his forehead as he listened to Austin's explanation. "Now what do we do?"

"Well, this one is pretty cute." Ashley held up her new friend, who by now was purring loudly enough for everyone to hear. How could she resist?

"Yeah, but at least we won't be taking a kitty home," Austin said. "Characters and animals and stuff don't go from Web site to Web site. Or home."

"Ah, but these ones do, internaut friends!"

Hello? So they weren't alone after all. They whirled around to see a woman dressed in blue bib overalls stepping their way, smiling and holding out her hand as she hovered over the kitten sea.

"Welcome to *LostKitty-dot-com.* You're just in time," she said, reaching out to shake their hands. "I'm Cindy, and we're in the middle of an adoption drive," she explained. "We're looking for good homes for all our adorable animals. Take little Checkers, for instance—"

Blink! She was holding out a kitten the way a stage magician would pull a rabbit out of a hat.

"Checkers is about six months old, black and white, and loves children. He's playful and hopes to find a family with active kids. He's available for adoption today."

"How did you do that?" Austin leaned in closer as if to see what kind of trick she was playing. Suddenly Checkers disappeared and a big brown cat took his place.

"Now, Izzy is older, maybe five or six. But she likes to play with her chew toy and would love to take a nap with you. Contact…"

And so on. Austin and his folks were looking around, no

doubt hoping to find a link that would take them out of there. But as far as Ashley was concerned, the kittens were too cute to leave.

"Excuse me." She didn't want to interrupt Cindy, but she had to know. "After my brother told my parents that characters can't go between Web sites, I thought you said these could. Is that right?"

"Ah yes." The woman smiled. "This site is specially set up for pet adoptions. The normal rules don't apply here."

"You mean…" Ashley held up her purring kitty.

"That's right. Take as many home as you want. Internet pets are especially easy to care for on the Outside. You save big on food and vet bills. And forget about litter boxes!"

"Hey, Austin, did you hear that?" Ashley turned to see where the others had wandered off to.

"Everyone should have a lifelike digital Internet pet from *www-dot-LostKitty-dot-com*," Cindy said.

By this time Ashley had collected three more kittens besides the one in her arms. One was sitting on each of her shoulders, and one was balancing on the top of her head. It didn't seem like too many to her. But her family was down on their hands and knees, digging through kittens to find a link.

"Right down here, Dad," Austin was saying. "I can even see the red glowing light!"

If she'd had her way, Ashley would have stayed a little

longer. They could still pick out a few more kitties. But she knew that if she didn't get over to the link in a second...

"Hey, wait a minute!" Cindy called. "The rest of you haven't picked out a kitten to take home!"

Austin waved before he disappeared with a *swoosh*. Even Ashley was ready to step through the link.

"I'm sorry, Ashley, but not now." Her dad shook his head at the sight of the kittens that had latched onto her. "Maybe—"

"Maybe Mom and Dad would like their own virtual kittens to take home?" The cat woman came by with a handful and placed several in their hands.

"Thanks, but we really can't." Mrs. Webster handed her kittens back with a weak smile. Mom had never really liked cats.

"Tell you what." Mr. Webster handed his back too. "We need to follow our son right now, but maybe we can swing by another time."

Ashley sighed and handed the four kittens back to Cindy, offering her own apology.

"Do you think you could hold these for me?"

The woman told her she would, while Ashley took her mom's hand.

"Don't forget to bookmark this site and come back often." Cindy juggled the small mound of kitty as she smiled and waved. "It's easy to get lost if you don't."

Ashley already knew that well enough, but she tried to sound cool. "Now we'll just step into the link together." She held her mom's and dad's hands as she stared down at the glowing link.

Only her mom held back. "I still think you should have checked the map, Tom."

Map or no map, Ashley stepped into the link.

CHAPTER 9

URL Don't Share

"This is getting more entertaining all the time."

Raven Zawistokowski leaned back in his office chair and clasped his hands behind his head. Maybe this wasn't going to be so hard after all. But he had to laugh at the sight of the two Webster kids and their parents, covered in virtual kittens.

Cute.

Good thing they had left behind a big, fat trail. The red trail in his locator program told him everything he needed to know, almost down to the footsteps they took, so that he could adjust to that level of detail if he wanted to. Their online session may have begun this time at *www.Austin-Webster.com,* but they hadn't stayed there long.

So the kid was probably showing his parents his site. How sweet. But having *them* online could only lead to more trouble. And their next hyperlink hadn't made much sense, until he noticed the Webster girl hugging an armload of kitty fur at *www.LostKitty.com.*

"Hmm." He glanced around his cubicle at the Normal Council on Civil Correctness and paused. No one knew about the photo he kept in the little walnut frame on his desk, tucked behind the picture of an endangered gray wolf. Not even Mattie, who knew everything that went on in the office. But he didn't dare peel back the edge of the top photo, not even for a quick peek.

Because if he did, the security camera behind him would show Mattie that he'd saved a photo of himself when he was ten years old, his arms around a fat tabby cat named Buster. Around here, Mr. Z couldn't risk being seen as too cute, or too soft. He had a job to do.

Forget about Buster! He shook his head and reminded himself not to say the words out loud. Mattie's microphone would pick them up, and she would wonder. Instead, he refigured the code he needed for deleting this threat to their mission.

Mattie's voice crackled over the intercom.

"Z! How's it going with your reprogramming? Are you ready to shut down the Webster threat?"

Mr. Z clicked back to the program that would help him clean things up, the way he had promised her. No sweat. No problem. No worries. Only thing was... Well, he didn't want to worry her with details. She didn't need to know the program was only in beta.

In other words, he'd never done this before.

But never mind that. He focused on the program and the two options.

1. Delete. (This command cannot be undone.)

2. Delete copy. (This command saves a version in another place.)

He made sure he checked the second option. The boss wanted them out of the Internet for good, not totally zapped. The only problem was, he wasn't quite sure what would happen to a *real* person when he used this program on them. It had worked before on Internet characters...most of the time. But real people who happened to be temporarily digital?

"Z! I want a report!"

"Right. Just a sec." He switched back to *www.LostKitty .com,* and for a moment he thought he could see Buster in the sea of lost cats on the site. He stared at the woman in blue bib overalls who was showing dozens and dozens of the animals, one after the other. Maybe...

No. He had a job to do, and there was only one way to do it. It was the Websters' fault for being places they shouldn't be, for messing with things they shouldn't be messing with, for poking their noses into some of the most creative programming he'd ever come up with. It wasn't his fault.

Two more clicks took him to the last place he had seen the family, and he zoomed in on the action. *There.*

For just a moment Ashley Webster held up one of the cutest kittens he'd ever seen. He couldn't delete the kitten too, could he?

"Come on." He tapped on his mouse. "Out of the way, kitty."

"Raven!" Mattie's voice screeched through his cubicle now, and he knew he didn't want her coming across the office to visit him in person. He jammed his finger down on the Talk button.

"I've got them," he told her. But in the three or four seconds it took his screen to refresh, the Websters had disappeared. The viewfinder blinked a message:

Targets: zero.

Instantly, he locked down the site, but it was too late. He hit his fist on the desk and looked back over his shoulder at the camera. Mattie would be checking on him by now.

"They linked out before I could transfer them, Mattie. But don't worry. I'm right on their tails."

And he knew he'd better be.

Austin pulled at his earlobes as he watched his dad pace around the bare Web site.

"We're obviously not going in the right direction." Mr. Webster wasn't saying anything they didn't already know.

Well, maybe this site was still under construction, or maybe it was a lost page. Austin wished he knew. All he could say was...

"Uh, I'm not sure *what* this place is."

The only sign of life was an old man in a rocking chair, rocking back and forth on a sort of porch that wasn't painted or finished—just like the rest of the site. The guy was holding the long, white box that would normally have hung at the top of the site so people could read where they were.

Yeah, this site was under construction all right. And Austin couldn't do a thing about it, especially since his good, old laptop was dead. Well, not *dead* dead—just the battery was dead. But for a family lost inside the Web, that was bad enough.

"Listen, sir," Ashley said very politely. "Couldn't you give us a little clue about where we are?"

"Name's URL. Watch where you step. That's all I can tell you."

"Don't you know even part of the address here?" Ashley tried again. "We'd love a look. Please?"

The guy shook his head and held the box so they couldn't read it, like a toddler who hadn't learned how to share yet. When Ashley crouched down to get a glance, he turned it away.

"We'll stop bothering you if you tell us how to get out of here." Mrs. Webster gave it a try. "You must know."

URL kept rocking and folded his arms across his chest, as if he was thinking.

"Oh, come on!" Even their mom had run out of patience. She stomped across the porch. "The least you could do is—"

She didn't finish her sentence as she dropped out of sight. *Boom!* One second she was there, stomping; the next she was gone.

Austin jumped over to where she had been. So that's why URL had told them to watch their step.

"I don't *see* any link," he said. Maybe the links in this place were lost.

There was only one way to find out.

CHAPTER 10

Dark. Damp. Lost.

Lost, loser, lostest! Ashley was standing in the dark, shivering in the water that lapped around her legs and wondering where they had linked to *this* time.

"Don't let go of my hand," she told her mother. But from the way her mom clamped down on Ashley's fingers, she guessed the chance of that was slim to none.

"Tom, where are we now?" Mrs. Webster's voice trembled in the dark.

And that was Dark with a capital D. Not the everyday kind of dark, the way it gets at night when you can hardly see. There are still streetlights and moonlight and shadows in that kind of dark.

This kind of dark was middle-of-the-jar-of-ink dark.

Close-my-eyes-and-blindfold-me-and-put-a-blanket-over-my-head dark.

Can't-see-my-hand-two-inches-from-my-face dark.

But just because they couldn't see a thing didn't mean they couldn't hear and feel and smell.

Ashley could hear the echo of water dripping all around their heads, plunking into the shallow puddle or lake that surrounded them.

She could feel a cold, musty draft against the back of her neck, her goose bumps running up and down like the mall escalator in downtown Normal.

And she could smell the deep, dark underground smell that told her they were stuck in a cave somewhere.

Lost again. But then, those were the only kinds of sites they'd been to lately.

"Okay, nobody move." Her dad's voice echoed all around. From the sound of it, Ashley guessed the ceiling had to be pretty high up.

"Ashley and I aren't going anywhere," said her mom. Ashley was ready to add her amen to that. "B-b-but we can't just k-k-keep standing here. This water is going to f-f-freeze our t-toes off."

"How ab-b-bout we all hang on to each other and start m-m-moving very slowly?" Ashley thought that was an okay idea. "Maybe we'll get to higher g-g-ground."

Either that or drop into a deep pool.

"Sounds g-g-good to me." Austin's teeth were chattering just as badly as hers.

So they made a single-file chain, holding on to one another's hands as they snaked their way through the cave. They hadn't taken more than three or four steps when Ashley heard a splash and a strange howl.

"YIIIII!" She could scream with the best of them, when she needed to. And now Ashley let loose with the shriek of a lifetime.

"Ashley!" their dad yelled.

Their mom yelled.

Austin yelled.

For one horrible moment Ashley thought they were done for. Maybe they'd linked to a monster Web site or something, and the horrible thing scratching at her leg was a bloodsucking bat, or even worse. Or was it a...

Kitty?

"Wait a minute." Ashley's heart was still racing as she picked up the wet ball of fur. But at least she knew what it was.

"Ashley!" Her mom grabbed Ashley's neck this time, probably feeling for a pulse. "Are you all right? What—"

"It's a kitty." Ashley held the little guy close as he dug in his claws. She would have dug in her claws too, if she had been in his place. "He must have followed us here."

Her dad sighed. "Well, I'm glad to hear we haven't been attacked. So can we link out again? We need to—"

"Shh!" This time it was Austin's turn to interrupt. "Did you hear that?"

Once again they stood absolutely still, listening to the drips and their steady breathing. And sure enough.

"Ladies and gentlemen…" A faint voice echoed down to them, growing louder as it came closer. "In a moment we'll be coming upon the Lost Sea, America's largest underground lake, here at *www-dot-lost-sea-cave-dot-com*."

The Lost Sea. So that was their "lost" link.

The tour guide's voice went on.

"We're now more than three hundred feet below the surface near the town of Sweetwater. And not only is this part of Tennessee's largest cave attraction, but the *Guinness Book of World Records* lists it as the world's largest underground lake. The part you'll see is four and a half acres, but we don't know how deep it really is.

"Yes? A question?"

They heard a mumbled echo from somebody in the tour group.

"Ah, no. You don't need to be concerned about that scream you heard. I'm sure it was just somebody back at the surface trying out the echo. It's easy to get your sounds turned around down here."

By this time the Websters could see the flicker of a flashlight from just behind a bend in the cave. A little more light glimmered across the surface of the lake. And from what Ashley could make out, the tourists were standing on some rocks a few feet from the shore.

"Hey!" Austin groaned and put up his hands. Ashley knew exactly how Gollum must have felt—that sorry cave creature in The Lord of the Rings. Her eyes were already so used to the dark, she had to hide from the light. The kitty—now on her head—hissed like an alien.

Or it must have looked that way to the tourists, who came unglued and started screaming even louder than Ashley had a few minutes back. One even jumped up on the tour guide's shoulders, which didn't work too well. And all of a sudden the guide didn't seem to want to be there either. The whole group of about ten people stood there dancing and screaming for a couple long seconds while Austin and Ashley and their parents tried to hold out their hands and tell them it was okay.

But that didn't help. The cave tourists turned and ran back up the way they'd come, yelling the whole way.

Ashley stood there watching as the lights faded out of sight.

"Should we go after them?" she wondered aloud. At least they knew the way now. Sort of.

"Even if we did," Austin mumbled, "we'd still need a light."

The strange thing was, the cave didn't seem quite as dark now as before. And when Ashley glanced down at the bottom of the lake, she noticed a faint gleam. One of the tourists had dropped a flashlight.

And there was only one way to get it.

CHAPTER 11

CtrL-ALt-DeLete

Mr. Z poked at the Brightness button on his computer screen.

"What is *wrong* with this thing?" he muttered and leaned all the way forward, as if that would help him see better in the dark.

He was glad he was here in the comfort of his cubicle and not lost inside the Web. Controlling everything from the Outside... Now that was the way to do it.

Only trouble was, things didn't always work out quite the way they were supposed to. He tapped on the screen, trying to get it to lighten up.

"Phooey." He nearly bit his tongue for saying it out loud. *Remember the security cam she had installed over your desk?* He glanced at his watch and slipped down into his office chair a few inches.

Mattie will appear in six, four, two...

"What's wrong here?" Mattie Blankenskrean breezed

around the corner, her purple silk shawl flying behind her like wings. "Why aren't you wrapping things up?"

Mr. Z sighed and didn't even try to click out of the black screen to someplace else. Times like this made him wonder why he didn't settle for a nice, safe job. Like a lion trainer or maybe a test pilot.

"Look, the site they're on is totally dark, okay?" He pointed at his screen. "And there's nothing wrong with my computer. I just can't see a thing."

"Well, isn't that lovely." She frowned as she looked over his shoulder. "But I suppose that's what you'd expect in a cave, right?"

Oh. He looked more closely at the URL, the Web address. He thought it had said something about a sea.

"My dear Mr. Raven Zawistokowski." Whenever she used his full name, he knew he was in trouble. "Perhaps it's a good time to review our progress. You did that with your students, did you not?"

"All the time," he mumbled.

"Pardon?" She might have pretended not to hear.

"I said yes, of course. Review away."

"You recall our purpose in sending you into Chiddix Junior High last year?"

He nodded as she went on.

"As I remember, you told me when you were hired that

you would have 'no problem at all' locating and confiscating the laptop computer and digital camera that allow the Webster children inside the Internet."

"I remember," he squeaked.

"But of course that didn't work out the way you expected, and the Websters have continued to enter the Web again and again. And each time they enter, they put our good work at risk. Isn't that the case?"

"That's the case." What else could he say?

"So when I allowed you to enter the Internet a short while back to take care of the situation, I assumed it would be taken care of. It was not. And when I allowed you to create a digital clone to take care of the situation, again it was not." Now she was counting things off on her fingers, and her cheeks were turning red. Not good signs.

"So that makes three separate occasions when you attempted to correct matters, and three separate occasions when you failed. Am I accurately describing things up to this point?"

Mr. Z thought back to the times in the eighth grade when his stepdad had grounded him for not getting straight As. Closing his eyes, he could see the man yelling at him the same way Mattie was yelling at him now.

"Yes sir," he blurted out before opening his eyes and realizing his mistake. "I mean yes. Just yes."

Mattie narrowed her eyes at him for a second and then pulled back and seemed to soften a bit.

"I'm sorry. I didn't mean to raise my voice. But you can understand my frustration. Really, we're trying to help the Websters stay safe, and it's not always easy to do. People don't appreciate what we do, as you know. There's very little thanks in this job."

You can say that again, he thought.

"Ah yes... There's very little thanks in this job," she repeated. "Did I say that already? So here's what I'm going to do."

He sighed. *Another chance?*

"I don't want you to waste any more time. Simply locate them as quickly as you can, and then shut down the entire site. I do it all the time."

He didn't want to correct her. But of course the Websters weren't exactly *characters* the way characters on a Web site were characters.

"Actually, there's a problem with that," he told her, barely whispering. "Shutting down the entire site would be too messy. People would notice if an entire site was down, and eventually someone would bring it back up, with the Websters still inside."

She had to agree.

"So I have to click on each person, one at a time," he

explained. "Then we can trash them and delete the files without leaving any fingerprints. No trace. It's better for everyone that way."

"All right." She sighed. "I didn't want it to come to this, but here we are. First we have to find them, though, and we're surely not going to find anyone in this black cave. Let's shed a little light on the picture, shall we?"

Mattie reached for the background controls, as if she had done this sort of thing before. He knew it was a bit of a show, but he let her. Sure enough...

"You see that?" A small light flickered at the bottom of the screen. *How about that.* It was a shadowy image of the Webster girl standing in the water and holding a flashlight in her upraised hand.

"There they are." Mattie smiled and looked away, seemingly pleased with her success. Whether or not she had actually done anything didn't matter.

Mr. Z looked closer and rolled his pointer directly over the flashlight.

But what was that—a kitten? He paused.

"All you do now is press control-alt-delete," she told him as she walked away. "Delete them now, while you have the chance. Unless you have a better plan, of course."

Mr. Z looked at the kitten once more, swallowed hard— and reached for the Delete key.

CHAPTER 12

Lost Cybercity

Okay, Austin didn't need his dead laptop to see the pattern now. From Lost Lake Resort to lost kitties. Lost URL and the Lost Sea.

Every place they'd been to had something that was lost, and by this time that was no surprise to anyone. The only question was, what was lost here?

The pop-up ads told him first.

"Lost City T-shirt specials!" A guy with an armful of bright, touristy stuff draped over his arm popped into the Web site from the side, and the Websters had to duck so he didn't nail them in the face. "One for eight dollars; two for fifteen!"

Ah, but that wasn't all. Another guy wearing a very cool-looking beanie swooped in from the other side. These Lost City survival hats were only twelve dollars when purchased online.

At first glance this didn't look like much of a city, lost or otherwise. They could see no skyscrapers or tall buildings. All that was left of the city were waist-high rock walls tumbled across a couple mountaintops. It looked to Austin as if someone had sliced the old walls in half with a huge machete. But it was for sure better than the cave.

"Ready to buy?" The hat sales guy showed off the knitted wool hats in blue and red and yellow triangle patterns. Actually, the pull-down earmuff flaps would have been great to fend off the wind that the Websters had suddenly stepped into. But just as Austin was thinking about seeing if the guy would take ten bucks, Ashley grabbed him by the arm and weakly steered him away.

"Sorry." Austin tripped on a rock outcropping and almost stumbled off the edge of a cliff. *Yikes!*

So this was the Lost City? Make that *very* lost. The rocky, wind-swept mountaintop, covered with ancient stone ruins, poked right up into the clouds. A mountain climber's paradise, as long as a person was dressed for it.

Austin and his family, on the other hand, were not. They huddled together to keep the wind off Ashley, who was soaked to the skin and shivering in the shadows of the lost city of Machu Picchu. Not even her kitten looked worse, and he looked like a drowned rat.

"My flashlight," Ashley mumbled, looking at her empty hand. "What happened to my flashlight?"

Austin didn't have an answer for that. But at least they didn't need it to find out more about this place. Buttons had popped up all around them like weeds in a spring lawn. Click here to learn more about Machu Picchu's history or about the Incas who built it. Here to learn more about the Peruvian Andes. See the temperature here. And check out vacations to the Incan ruins.

But right now Austin had other things on his mind, like his lost family and his soaking wet sister. *What now?*

"I think I'm g-getting the hang of this Internet place now," their dad told them. His teeth were chattering too, though he was dry except for his feet.

At least the sun was… Well, not anymore. A herd of dark clouds rushed up over the mountain, covering them in a blanket of damp fog.

"I think we need to find an e-mail link out of here." Austin wasn't worried about getting back to the right e-mail address just now. Forget the Lost Lake Resort. Anywhere Outside would be fine.

But Mr. Webster shook his head. "I think I can find us the right way out of here," he insisted, but he must have changed his mind pretty quickly when he saw how blue Ashley was getting. "What about that plane up there? Is that another link?"

Austin could barely make out the wording—something to

do with *Lost Flights*. Well, maybe that would have been a fine way out, if they could have reached it. But right now—

"Tom!" Their mom had noticed Ashley's blue fingers and shivering too.

"Okay." Mr. Webster pulled out his wallet, fished out a credit card, and handed it to Austin. "Go buy us a pile of those T-shirts and wool hats—anything else you can find—and we'll try to get your sister warmed up."

Actually, that was the best idea Austin had heard in a while. Ashley was going to freeze to death up here on this mountain. So five minutes later he stumbled back with twenty Lost City 100-percent-cotton T-shirts, six "I (Heart) Machu Picchu" hooded sweatshirts, and four of those cool, woolen Andean-Indian beanies with the ear flaps and all the wild colors.

"You want the receipts?" he asked his dad before glancing again at the *Lost Flights* link. The plane didn't look like a jet, just a little propeller-type plane. Well, at least it was going someplace. Wouldn't that be better than being stuck up here on this freezing, foggy, windy mountaintop? Even bundled up in layers of souvenir T-shirts and sweatshirts, Austin was still shivering.

Lost flights, huh? Once Ashley and her cat had warmed up a bit, that just might be the way to go.

CHAPTER 13

PLane Mistake

⌐⊕

"Amelia Earhart." The pilot of their small plane held out her hand with a warm smile and nodded at the serious-looking man seated next to her. "That's my navigator, Fred Noonan. Welcome to *www-dot-lostflights-dot-com*."

Considering the site they had just come from, Ashley didn't mind the noise. Okay, so she could hardly hear Amelia's shout above the roar of the powerful twin engines. But at least the wind was outside now, and the warmth was inside.

"Sorry about the mess," the pilot apologized. "Fred and I would have cleaned up a bit if we'd known we were going to have visitors."

Still bent over his map, Fred didn't move.

"No time to be entertaining, Amelia." He talked out of the side of his mouth without looking at them. Maybe he had a point: The plane had room for the pilot and a navigator, but they sure weren't expecting to carry any stowaways.

"I'm sorry. We didn't mean to—" Ashley started to apologize, but Amelia wouldn't have it.

"Forget it. I'm here to help. That's a cute kitty."

Amelia reached out to pet the cute kitty, who was curled up in a dry Machu Picchu sweatshirt, doing much better.

"He likes you." Ashley smiled. Her parents looked much calmer too, now that they were away from that horrible Lost City. *Brrr.*

Austin seemed pretty jazzed about this new site. "Wow! A real Lockheed Electra," he said. "And look at all the links! *Lost Voyages* and *Lost Continents* and *Lost Colonies…*" He reached out to touch one of the links, but Fred growled at him.

"Look but don't touch, kid."

The pilot chose then to launch into a little speech about the site.

"So, I'm Amelia Earhart, 1897–1937, American aviatrix. Don't you like that word, *aviatrix?* Kind of rolls off the tongue."

"Come on, Amelia." Fred obviously didn't like giving background information to internauts. "Why don't you tell them we're lost?"

"First woman to cross the Atlantic, 1928. First person to fly alone from Hawaii to California, 1935. Almost made it around the world, but in July 1937 was lost in the mid-Pacific somewhere between New Guinea and Howland Island."

Oh-oh. That kind of lost. The engines droned on, and the Websters looked at one another as Amelia Earhart turned back to flying her plane.

"I still think it's more beautiful up here than anywhere else," Amelia said quietly, and Ashley thought she saw a tear in the pilot's eye. But this site was getting kind of creepy now. Maybe they should have stayed back in Machu Picchu.

"We're losing altitude, Amelia." Fred delivered bad news. "Maybe you should try the Coast Guard cutter again."

Amelia picked up her radio microphone.

"KHAQQ calling the *Itasca*," she spoke with calm control as she tapped one of the instruments with her finger. The gas gauge, maybe? "We must be on you but cannot see you. Gas is running low."

Amelia was already wrestling with the steering, trying her best to stay on course. Ashley's mom clutched at Mr. Webster as the plane pitched and dipped in a sudden downdraft. Did they have airsick bags on this plane?

"Sorry, folks." Amelia didn't seem to be giving up anytime soon, even though she knew the ending to her story. "I wish it didn't have to happen this way. I think it may be a good time for you to bail out."

"Way past time," muttered Fred.

"I'm very sorry if we shouldn't have come," Ashley said.

Fred looked up from the instruments he'd been eyeing.

"You seem like a nice kid," he told her. "So let me tell you something: You're being watched, and I don't mean by people visiting our Web site."

"What do you mean, *watched?*" asked Austin.

Fred checked his instruments again and pointed down at one.

"See this? This is the number of hits on our Web site. And we've been clicked on 250 times since you got here."

"Two hundred and fifty!" Ashley whistled.

"I may not know exactly where we are," Fred said, "but something's up, and it doesn't look good to me."

"Hey!" Austin smiled. "I'll bet Jessi found us. Go, Jessi!"

Ashley and Austin's parents looked at each other as if this was the lifeline they needed.

But Fred wasn't smiling. "I don't know who this Jessi is, but the person doing all the looking right now is..." He checked his instrument one more time. "*NCCC-dot-org.*"

Austin's smile disappeared, and their parents looked confused.

"Do you know anyone with those initials, dear?" their mom asked their dad.

"Thanks, Mr. Noonan." Ashley stood up. "We've got to go."

"Do you know who that is, Ashley?" Her mother stopped her. But there wasn't time for that now.

"We'll explain later, Mom." The color in Austin's face had drained, and Ashley didn't have to ask why.

"One of those links, Austin. Let's go."

He nodded and sniffed at one of the links he had almost touched earlier.

"This one smells like Italian food."

Ashley didn't understand how her brother could have an appetite now, but she was happy to try the link. With one last wave, she followed Austin and her parents and bailed out of the plane, realizing too late that she'd forgotten the kitty.

CHAPTER 14

Meeting Marco

Thunk. In an instant Austin knew they weren't in Amelia Earhart's plane anymore. This ground felt solid.

Way solid. *Ouch!*

Raaaahk! The grunt sounded like the Loch Ness monster clearing its throat, or maybe their Papa Reuben blowing his nose in the morning. But unlike their grandpa, the camel making the noises didn't look too pleased that the Websters had literally dropped in.

"Whew, there, big fella!" Austin fanned his face to keep from passing out. "Anybody ever told you about breath mints?"

He guessed camels didn't eat that sort of thing. Too bad. A couple of the nearby animals kept up their snorting and slobbering and throat-clearing noises. *Lovely. Really adds to the place.*

Austin had never been anywhere so dusty. As in, dusty ground, dusty camels, dusty tents. Dust swirled around the

Websters in puffs, getting in their faces and noses and eyes. Dust got in their mouths, too, and it tasted dry and gritty.

At least the sky was big, sort of like the sky in the middle of a big cornfield after everything had been cut after harvest. And the land around them on this site stretched out for miles and miles as far as he could see in every direction. The winds seemed to come all the way from China, and along the way, those same winds had picked up the dinner smells he'd noticed coming from the link in the plane.

Austin's stomach growled like a radio-beacon locator that had found its signal. And as he and his family stood there trying to decide what to do, a college-age guy stepped around the corner of his tent with a black kettle in his arms.

"Oh!" The guy dropped the kettle when he saw the Websters, and the water sloshed everywhere, making a big mud puddle.

"Marco!" a man yelled from behind the tent. "Tell me you didn't just drop the cooking water."

"Sorry, Uncle Matteo. But you should see this."

A minute later Marco was joined by his uncle and another man. A handful of rough-looking camel drivers also pushed in behind them to see what was going on.

"Finally, you've arrived!" Uncle Matteo, a dark-eyed man with more hair on his face than on the top of his head, grabbed each of them by the shoulders and gave them a kiss on both cheeks.

"Well—" Austin started to say something, but their hosts were too busy hugging and kissing them.

"I'm Niccolo Polo." This man was the tallest of the three and was obviously in charge. "You're most welcome here. Though I must say that, like my son, I'm a little surprised."

Aha. So this would be Marco Polo's dad.

"We're sorry for dropping in like this," Mrs. Webster apologized for them.

"Yeah," added Austin. "We would have called ahead, but we didn't have your number."

The three men looked at him blankly for a moment before a grin broke out on Marco's face.

"These are internauts, father. They're programmed differently."

Niccolo Polo stroked his beard and studied them a moment before nodding his head as if he understood.

"I suppose internauts are better than nothing. We should assume the other ninety-six will be arriving soon."

"Pardon?" Now it was Austin's turn to act confused. But the Polos weren't explaining just yet.

"We'll talk it over later." Uncle Matteo led the way back to their tent. "For now we eat!"

And a short while later, all the Websters had to admit that

Marco Polo and his family ate pretty well. Inside the tent they'd rolled out thick woven rugs and set up a short-legged picnic table piled high with steaming bowls of noodles.

"What do you think?" Uncle Matteo seemed especially proud of their meal. "Maybe it could use a little tomato sauce, but everyone back home in Italy is going to go crazy over this stuff. We got the idea from China."

"So the Chinese really did invent spaghetti?" Austin thought it would be a factoid to have handy for the next Knowledge Bowl competition—if he ever got out of here to compete again.

"Well, some people on the Outside don't believe it." Uncle Matteo leaned forward as if he was giving the Websters the inside scoop. "But it's true. And the book my nephew is going to write won't even tell the *half* of the story!"

He slapped Marco on the back and laughed.

"I've heard some people say that Marco Polo never really made it to China at all," Ashley said as her plate was dished high with noodles.

Uh-oh. For a moment everyone went silent, and they could hear the wind whistling outside the tent. A camel snorted in the distance. Uncle Matteo stared hard at them, and Austin wondered if the man might pull out some kind of sword.

CHAPTER 15

PoLo NoodLing

Ashley had just been trying to make conversation. But nobody seemed to like her question.

"Marco Polo never really made it to China?" whispered Uncle Matteo. He repeated it again and then burst out laughing.

Marco and Niccolo and Matteo nearly rolled on the floor at what they must have thought was a joke, and the Websters politely joined in.

"That's about—*ha-ha*—the silliest thing—*ha-ha*—I've ever heard." Niccolo was wiping the tears from his eyes.

"I'm sorry," Ashley tried to backtrack. "I just thought—"

"You must have read some crazy newfangled history Web site, is what I'm thinking." Uncle Matteo ladled an extra heaping helping of spaghetti noodles on everybody's plate. "Written by some fancy professor someplace who's never even been here."

"Excuse me?" Mr. Webster raised his hand. "Where exactly *is* here?"

Uncle Matteo laughed again. "Is a joke, no?"

"I don't think they know, Uncle." Marco took a bite of his pasta as his uncle wrinkled his bushy eyebrows and shrugged.

"Well, I would think a smart internaut missionary like you would know where he has been sent. So look around you at Central Asia. Here we are at *www-dot-MarcoPolosLost Christians-dot-com.* This is the real thing, right, Marco? Of course, right."

Ashley wasn't sure what he meant by "Lost Christians," but Marco nodded as his uncle went on with the story.

"In year of our Lord 1271, brave explorers and traders Matteo and Niccolo Polo returned to China with Niccolo's seventeen-year-old son, Marco, to visit the great Kublai Khan, master of Mongolia, northern China, Tibet, and soon, southern China."

"I'm sure they've heard this story, Matteo." His brother tried to interrupt, but Matteo wasn't done yet.

"These internauts don't even know where we are! I will tell the rest of the story!" Matteo leaned into the table once more and lowered his voice. "The part you do not always hear is the great favor the Khan asked of the Polo brothers before they left China the first time."

He puffed up his chest as if he was imitating the great ruler.

"The Khan told us to bring him one hundred missionaries from our country—one hundred missionaries to explain our gospel to him and his people. And if we did this for him"—by this time everyone was into the story, leaning in to hear every word—"he and his people would follow Jesus!"

Uncle Matteo made as if he were washing his hands in the air, as if he were wrapping up his story. But—

"But where are the missionaries?" Austin asked.

Uncle Matteo stabbed the air with his finger.

"My question exactly! When we got home, we asked and we asked. And do you know how many missionaries joined us on our return trip? Two!"

By that time Uncle Matteo's cheeks had turned as red as spaghetti sauce.

"That's not quite one hundred." Of course, Ashley's brother could do the math.

"No! And you know what? Those two went running home with their tails between their legs at the first sign of trouble. What kind of missionaries were they, I ask? This is why we're so happy you have shown up. Now we have four more missionaries, and only ninety-six to go."

"Oh, wait a minute." Mr. Webster started to explain. "We're not—"

"Tut, tut, tut." Uncle Matteo raised his hand. "It is time to eat now; we talk later. You will need your strength. We still have a long way to go before we reach the Kublai Khan."

Austin grinned across the table at his sister. The noodles were good and the Polos seemed nice, even if Uncle Matteo was a character. If it weren't for all the dust and the nasty camels, maybe they wouldn't mind being Web missionaries to China.

Ashley giggled into her pasta, but when she looked up— zoot!—she blinked once and completely disappeared.

"Ashley?" Their mom dropped her fork and jumped up. "What happened to Ashley?"

Austin looked around to check for links. Nothing. Ashley hadn't touched anything that would have taken her someplace else. *What in the world?*

"This is normal for internauts?" Marco stood up too.

"No, not this." Austin stepped over to see if she had left anything behind when they heard another *zoot!* And just like that, his mother was gone.

"Austin?" His dad looked at him, but Austin could only shake his head in reply. Something was not right here, and he had a feeling he knew where this trouble was coming from.

Zoot! The bowl of spaghetti right next to him flickered

and was gone. If someone had been aiming for him, that person had just missed.

"Dad! Under the—"

Zoot! Mr. Webster disappeared before he could take cover.

Only Marco seemed to realize what was going on. He grabbed Austin by the wrist as they stumbled outside. And before Austin could react, Marco had shoved him under one of the camels standing by the tents.

"Don't move!" hissed Marco, just before he himself was zapped.

CHAPTER 16

Internetted

This is bad. Austin tried to breathe under the full weight of the camel, which wasn't so easy since it had lowered itself on top of him. At least the sand was kind of soft. But if Austin came out of this alive, he would smell like a camelhair rug.

And that wasn't the worst of it.

Austin almost wanted to step out into the open so he could get zapped on purpose. Because if his mom and dad and Ashley were gone… Well, what was he doing here by himself?

"I should be where they are," he whispered.

And now his leg was asleep where it was jammed underneath the camel, next to his laptop. Like a lightning storm that had passed by, the zooting had stopped a few minutes ago.

"Marco?" he yelled toward the tents.

"Polo!" came the response from behind one of them.

So Austin crawled out, wiggled his leg, and tried again.

"Marco?"

"Polo!" The young explorer came around the corner. So he hadn't disappeared like the rest!

"There you are!" Austin looked around and over Marco's head. "I thought they got you, too. Do you think they're gone now?"

"Excuse me?" Marco Polo stared at him blankly. "You seem only a little familiar. Please tell me who you are and what you are talking about."

Austin tried to explain, but he couldn't get past Marco's blank stare. "I said I wondered if you got zapped too. Only I guess you didn't disappear. You just got your memory erased— is that it?"

"My memory is fine. You're just not part of it." Marco sniffed the air and leaned closer. "But if you don't mind my saying so, you smell a bit...er...musty."

Austin sighed. *That's what you get for hiding under a camel.*

"Let me talk to your dad and your uncle. Maybe they'll remember."

But Niccolo and Matteo Polo simply looked at each other and shrugged when Austin told them his story.

"Strange internauts tell strange tales, don't they?" Uncle Matteo scratched his head and brought out the same bowls they had been using for dinner before the zap attack. "I wonder where you came from. But here, you'll stay for dinner, no?"

At least that part of the Web site remained the same.

"Sorry." Austin held his stomach. "I'm still stuffed from the last spaghetti feed."

"Spaghetti?" Uncle Matteo paused for a moment, turned his head to the side, and shrugged. "I don't know *spaghetti*. And I don't remember you. For that matter I don't remember anything you're talking about."

"I'm Austin Webster." Austin thought he would try one more time. "My sister, Ashley, was here too. And my parents. You called us the...the missionaries."

"Missionaries?" Uncle Matteo looked even more puzzled, and when his mouth moved again, his words didn't quite match up, like the words came out a split-second later. "We don't believe it's healthy to force religious beliefs on indigenous cultures. We must respect diversity in all its forms."

What? That was sure weird, like watching a video with a delayed soundtrack, or a foreign film with English dubbed in. Somebody had been doing some quick work on this Web site while Austin had been hiding. And the results weren't good in more ways than one. It sure seemed to Austin like the work of the NCCC.

Marco didn't quite know what an "indigenous" culture is, so his uncle had to explain that it means natives or people who already live in a certain place, like the people of China and

Mongolia. The whole time he sounded more like an encyclopedia than the jolly Uncle Matteo who had first welcomed Austin and his family to their Web campsite.

"But what about the one hundred missionaries that the Kublai Khan asked you to bring back to him?" Austin wondered if that part of this site had been wiped clean too.

Sure enough, all he got back was another blank stare.

"I don't know anything about missionaries," Uncle Matteo told him. "But perhaps you'd like some tofu? It's a nutritious alternative to meat, rich in protein, B vitamins, and iron. Tofu is also an excellent source of calcium."

Well, that was all very nice, but right now Austin wasn't sure he could handle soybean JELL-O. One thing was sure, though: He knew he'd be sick if he found out that any more of the Marco Polo site had been rewritten. Not that it couldn't be fixed and returned to normal. But he'd need his computer up and running before he could try that again. Austin patted his poor machine. In the meantime, he'd better find his parents and Ashley before anything else happened.

But where to look?

"Your parents...your parents..." Marco wore an odd look on his face, as if he was trying to remember something but couldn't quite. Maybe the NCCC had missed something.

"You know where they went?" asked Austin, but Marco

suddenly held his head and swayed back and forth. Did he have a headache?

"It's like a dream." Marco glanced at a couple of links near the edge of their tent. Then he reached out to one of them, paused, and then turned to the other.

"They didn't hit any link." Austin didn't know if he could explain to a Web-site character, or even to himself, what had happened to Ashley and his folks. But Marco stiffened when he got close to the second link—a glowing blue button about the size of a stop sign.

"I know they didn't," he whispered. "But this is where you need to go right now. To be safe."

Austin held off for just a second, wondering what part of Marco's memory was telling him to hyperlink Austin to *www .Rigatelli-Pasta.com*.

"Bring me some noodles if you come back this way," Marco added. "I miss them, and I'm not so sure about that tofu."

CHAPTER 17

Virtual Pasta Inspector

"Fifty-four thousand farfallone for Frankfurt!" a man in an emerald green suit sitting at a computer screen shouted out for everyone to hear. He probably assumed everyone knew that farfallone is bowtie-shaped pasta.

"Fifty-four thousand farfallone!" Another green-suited guy standing on a platform yelled even louder, his voice echoing throughout the factory. "Ring the bell, Antonio!"

BONGGG!

A third guy with a big mallet seemed to be having a good time with a Chinese gong. The instrument fit right in at the noisy Italian pasta site.

Make that the *very* Italian pasta site. At the top of the screen, *www.Rigatelli-Pasta.com* danced in large letters like an out-of-control wedding guest. And it was hard to miss the red, white, and green Italian flags flapping, or the nutty aroma put out by all the pasta-making machines pouring out long strings of spaghetti, vermicelli, and elbow macaroni. Between the green-suited order takers shouting out each new order, the clanking machinery, and the gong, Austin wondered that everyone on this site wasn't deaf.

"Have you seen a girl about my age, maybe with her mom and dad?" Austin asked the nearest worker.

"What's that?" The middle-aged man stopped and held a hand to his ear.

"I said..." Austin started to repeat his question.

"Seventy-seven thousand spiralini, says Savannah!" came the shout.

The man shook his head.

BONGGG!

By then another pasta machine had started up, only this one was making cone-shaped noodles. *Clickety-clickety. Fwoosh!*

Austin sighed and asked his question again, but the man in the green suit shrugged and raised his hands.

"Sorry, pal. I've been working on this Web site for five years, and I can't hear a thing."

Well, that figures. But Austin couldn't give up. At least he still had his laptop. If he could find some way to power it up, he might be able to work his way out of this pasta mess and find his family. Until then, though, he had to wonder why Marco Polo had wanted him to come here.

He poked around a bit, passing the gong and the hollering order takers, passing ear-bending machines spitting out 142 varieties of pasta. Shaped pasta and tube pasta. Stringy noodles and ribbon noodles. Soup pasta and pasta to be stuffed. Asian noodles and SpaghettiOs. Rotini and spiralini, manicotti and penne, tuffoli and stringozzi…

"It's the Web inspector!" hollered one of the workers, and they scurried around as if someone had set off a fire alarm.

"This way, sir." A girl in a green suit took Austin by the arm and led him to a shiny, stainless-steel machine that huffed and puffed and shook the floor like a washing machine with a bunch of tennis shoes caught on one side during the spin cycle.

"Looks great to me," he told her, "but I'm not the—"

"That's what we like to hear," she interrupted him and picked up a steaming dish of tiny, sea shell–shaped pasta covered with a nice tomato sauce. "Try some of this cavatelli. You can rate it one to ten using those buttons on the right."

Well, even after all he'd eaten at the last site, Austin couldn't say no. The fiori were good too, and so were the gnocchi. He was glad he only had to eat them, not pronounce their cool Italian names. And after each sample, someone else in a green suit would pop up from nowhere with another sample for him to try.

"You sure you want me to eat *all* these?" Austin asked.

"As long as you say nice things about us on your *www-dot-ProfessionalPasta-dot-com* Web site."

"Wait a minute." Austin held up his hands. "These samples are great, but I'm not who you think I am. I'm just here looking for my sister and parents."

His host's eyes grew wide, and she snatched Austin's fork out of his hand just as he was about to take a bite of the wagon wheel–shaped pasta.

"Well, why didn't you say so?"

"I tried, but no one's listened till now. Sorry."

With all the samples he'd tried, Austin almost felt as if he'd have to be rolled out of there.

"The pasta was super tasty, though," he added.

"Hmm." The girl in the green suit didn't look too happy anymore. Suddenly she glanced up for a moment as if noticing that the wind had changed or a storm was about to hit.

And, boy, did it. Austin looked up as all the pasta workers dove for cover under their pasta machines. But Austin couldn't move fast enough before he felt a kind of tingling on the top of his head, like static. It reminded him of the times he'd rubbed a balloon on his hair until it stood on end.

He knew it was too late for him now. The NCCC had caught up with him at last.

Zoot!

CHAPTER 18

Worse Than Lost

Ashley didn't want to cry anymore, so she held her head in her hands and prayed. What else could she do? This was no Web site, with links or an e-mail section. No, if ever there was a dead end, this was it.

"I'm really, really, really sorry," she mumbled to her parents. "I never knew there was such a horrible place as this."

"It's not your fault, Ashley." Her dad paced the little platform once more. "It was nothing you did."

Easy for him to say. But she didn't mind him trying to make her feel better.

"Well, dear," her mom told her, "like you said, somebody must have *put* us here in this Internet trash can."

"That's right." Her dad rocked the platform. "And if somebody put us in, somebody can take us back out. We'll talk to the manager, if that's what it takes."

Well, that sounded hopeful. But who could the manager

be? Her dad had to know there was nobody here to complain to. Ashley couldn't see any way out.

Their small platform started to tip again, sort of like the floating platform anchored out in the swimming area at Lake Winnebago, though this platform was no bigger than a garage door. For sure, they didn't want to end up back in the Internet rubbish soup, where they had landed just a few minutes earlier.

"Please be careful, Tom." Mrs. Webster balanced herself right in the middle of the makeshift raft. "You know what that mess is like."

Don't remind me, thought Ashley. After slogging through knee-deep pools of castoff Web-site programming and files, she had wiped most of the sticky stuff off her shoes. But soggy bits of slimy code still stuck to her pant legs, along with spaghetti from the Polo site. Even her flashlight from the cave had somehow turned up here, though of course it couldn't help them.

Too bad. It didn't do Ashley any good to hold her nose. The rotten smell had soaked into everything. Who would have thought old digital things could smell so nasty?

The photos are the worst, she thought, *with all their colors running into each other and making a horrible, gooey, grayish-black mess.* They were like pools of digital maple syrup poured out all over the floor. Spreadsheets and other stray numbers flickered weakly as the last life leaked out of them. Some quivered and jerked in their final moments. Ashley had to look away.

But that was nothing compared to Ashley and her parents.

"Mom," she squeaked. "Do I look as bad as you?"

Okay, so that wasn't the nicest way to put it. But her mother didn't seem to mind, and she took Ashley's hand as they sat together on their life raft. Mrs. Webster's hair drooped, and her face had gone blurry. And everything that had once been in color was now black and white and gray.

Ashley's blue jeans?

Gray.

Her purple sneakers?

Ditto.

And so on. They had been turned into characters from a fuzzy, old black-and-white movie. And if this was the inside of a giant trash bucket, then...

"I think I know what's going on here," Ashley told them as she took a shallow breath and rubbed her nose. She wished she wasn't right, but she felt sure she was. "We've been—"

SPLASH! Something fell out of the ceiling and dropped right into the soup just inches from their raft, sending a wave of trash washing over them.

Gross.

Ashley held on to her parents as they bobbed to the top of a wave. And now there was no doubt who had dropped in on them. That was good news in a way…and bad news in another way.

"Grab my hand!" Ashley yelled to her brother. She and her dad would have tipped the raft over if her mother hadn't jumped to the other side to balance them out.

Austin looked up at Ashley like a drowning kitten as he sank down into a chest-deep pond of murky code and damaged files. He held up his laptop for them to take first. And between Ashley and her father, they managed to drag Austin up over the edge of the platform to safety. He lay on his back and panted for a moment to catch his breath.

"Sorry to drop in on you like this." He grinned weakly. And even though nothing was funny about this place, Ashley had to giggle too. "Would have been here earlier. But I wasn't sure I wanted to be trashed."

Trashed.

The word sounded so final. But of course that had to be what had happened. They'd been trashed, just like the floating bits of software and code, the PDFs, the JPEGs, the MP3s, and odd little souvenirs from those last sites they'd visited. Maybe those bits had been zapped too.

"At least we're still together." Her father pulled at the sleeve of his once red shirt that now was a dull gray. "And if we can still talk to and see each other, do you think that means we're not *totally* trashed? Maybe just halfway there?"

Hard to tell. But the terrible thought crossed Ashley's mind that something much worse *hadn't* happened to them.

The trash hadn't been emptied.

Yet.

Mr. Z paused with his finger over the Delete button, wondering one more time if there was another way.

But he had no one else to experiment on. No other way to find out if the Websters would be deleted in real life when he deleted them on the Internet. He looked up at the poster above his computer.

"Give Peace a Chance," it said.

Great idea. Was his job here really doing that? One thing he knew: If Mattie found him sitting at his desk without this problem under control, the office wouldn't be very peaceful.

At least with no way out of the trash can, the Websters weren't going anywhere. The boy would have used his computer by now if it were still working. That meant Mr. Z had plenty of time to go searching for the cute kitty he'd last seen in Amelia Earhart's plane. Because one thing was certain: Whatever else anyone said about Raven Zawistokowski, no one could say he was cruel to animals.

So he checked on the Websters one more time, making sure they were safely on the raft he'd placed there for them. *Good.* Now just a quick check on the kitty, and then he'd get right back to deal with things.

CHAPTER 19

Trashed

"This is the trash, all right." Austin looked down at his gray blue jeans.

"And there's really no way out?" his father asked.

"There would have been," Austin replied, "if we just had some battery power in my laptop."

"You're sure it doesn't work?" His mom already knew the answer. She'd seen him try to fire up his computer—and the blank screen when it didn't turn on. There wasn't enough juice left to fire up a digital clock, let alone e-mail them back to the Outside.

Austin knew none of them would care where they went now, so long as it wasn't here.

"At least the memory pack is fine." He pulled a small module about the size of a deck of cards from the side of the computer and then carefully plugged it back in. That was the brains of the machine. "It's only the battery that's bad. It needs more charge, and I'm not sure it can hold one anymore."

Austin unplugged the battery and held it up. The tiny light on the side that used to be red barely glowed. He looked up and shook his head, then he noticed the flashlight resting beside his mother on the raft.

Wait a minute.

Ashley looked at him just then. "Are you thinking what I'm thinking?" she asked him.

Well, Austin wasn't sure what *she* was thinking, but his idea just might work. The only trick would be connecting the batteries, but maybe he could work that out.

The keyword here was *maybe,* but that didn't stop him from grabbing the flashlight and popping out the batteries. The first two held nearly a full charge. The third had less. The fourth showed nearly half, but would it be enough?

Austin wasn't sure how the flashlight had made it here with all the other digital stuff. Maybe the NCCC had accidentally deleted it back at *www.lost-sea-cave.com.* Whatever the case, he had no idea if stringing together a handful of batteries from a deleted flashlight would work, but stranger things had happened online. And if it did—*zing!*—Austin's computer would be back in action, ready to send them wherever they wanted to go.

Maybe.

This time nobody argued about whether they should e-mail themselves back to the campground or back to their home in Normal or to Fred's Diner in Albuquerque, New Mexico. Anyplace Outside would be very, very nice.

"You sure this is going to work, son?" asked Austin's dad. "Because if we don't get out of here soon..."

They all knew they were close to being deleted for good. Austin didn't even want to think about it.

"Well..." All Austin could do was add another battery to the chain and hold it together as best as he could to make sure they all connected.

"It'll work." Ashley sounded sure of herself. "And when it does, Jessi will be so glad to see us again."

Austin hit his laptop's On button, held his breath, and waited to hear the cheery welcome chime.

Nothing.

"Ohh," his sister groaned, but nobody was quite ready to give up yet—even when one of the batteries slipped out of Austin's hands and fell overboard.

"Great!" Austin bit his lip. Down to three.

"It's okay," Ashley told him as she helped line up their remaining batteries. "It'll still work."

One more double-check, and he counted down again.

"Three, two, one..."

Bing-bong!

Their dad pumped his fist at the sound, and their mom clapped, but Austin wasn't celebrating yet. While Ashley held the batteries in place, he bent his ear over the computer like a doctor over a heart-attack patient.

"Isn't it working?" Ashley asked.

"Yeah…barely." As it finally started up, Austin pointed at the blinking red words in the corner of the screen: *You are now operating on reserve power. Shutdown in sixty seconds.*

Was that enough time to e-mail them somewhere Outside? Probably not. All Austin could manage was a quick adjustment to the Web browser, highlighting all their files and hitting the big blue arrow in the control bar that said Back.

He held his breath and squinted, waiting. Nothing. So he hit the arrow again.

And again.

And again.

Et cetera.

"Did it work?" whispered Ashley after Austin had tried eight times.

Not yet. But as the screen on his laptop flickered out for good, Austin felt the faintest of tingles and heard an even fainter *pop-pop-pop.*

CHAPTER 20

Road to Where?

"Brrr." Ashley shivered and tried to breathe, but she couldn't quite open her eyes—until someone grabbed her hand and dragged her out into the open.

"*There* you are!" Austin held her by the shoulders so she wouldn't trip. So this time it was *her* turn to be rescued.

"Thanks." She straightened up and tried to stand on her own, but at first it took her dad on one side and Austin on the other to keep her from falling. Her legs still felt like overcooked noodles.

"You took the long way," explained Austin. Then she understood that she had been the last one to hyperlink to... wherever they had ended up.

"Where are we?" Ashley wondered aloud.

"I'm not exactly sure." Austin shook his head. "I haven't been able to spot an address yet. The dust is making it tough to see."

Ashley shaded her face and looked out at the miles of open desert. In a way it looked a lot like *www.MarcoPolos LostChristians.com*. Burnt brown hills shimmered in the distance, and a rocky trail under their feet snaked through low hills.

"So we're still lost?" she asked.

"I'm not sure I'd say that." Austin grinned as he tugged at his *red* shirt. "At least we're not deleted anymore."

"Ah, living color," said their dad. Well, everybody could smile at *that*. Lost, okay. Deleted, no way.

Speaking of deleted, Ashley couldn't help worrying. "But how do we know the person who deleted us before isn't going to try it again?"

"We don't," Austin answered. "We've got to move fast."

"Perhaps we should find Marco Polo," suggested their mom. "He seemed like a nice young man. Do you think his camp is around here somewhere?"

"That's the first place they'd find us." Austin shook his head. "I think we'd get zapped again more quickly than before. And anyway, I'm not sure he's here."

"Austin's right." Mr. Webster had his take-charge voice back. "We'd better find some cover in this desert. Someplace to hide for now."

Or better yet, an e-mail link out of there. It certainly wouldn't hurt to look for one now that Austin's computer was once more officially dead—at least until they could get it a new battery.

"Tom." Their mom's voice sounded tired. "I don't care what we do, but I need to get out of this sun."

Ashley tried to swallow, but she started to cough from the dust. Ahead of them lay mountains. Behind, four men had nearly come up on them. One staggered as he clung to his friend's arm.

"Marco?" Ashley yelled.

But instead of replying right away, the travelers stopped in their tracks.

"Who's there?" asked the man who had been stumbling. He looked to the left and then the right, as if crossing a busy street. Even under his head covering and robe, Ashley thought he looked familiar. Except for the sunglasses, he looked kind of like a monk of some sort.

"I think I've seen that guy before," she whispered to her brother as the men stepped nearer. Still the middle-aged man didn't look straight at them, even when their dad reached out his hand.

"Tom Webster, my wife, Evelyne, and our kids, Austin and Ashley." He wiggled his fingers for a moment when the traveler didn't shake his hand, and then went on. "We're from Normal. From…Outside."

"Rabbi Saul of Tarsus." The stranger bowed slightly. "Forgive me. My friends and I don't often find internauts on this road."

"The road to…?" Mr. Webster asked, but Ashley could have told him by now.

"Damascus." He pulled off his sunglasses and blinked. "You want some advice, internauts? Keep your Tropic Ray sunglasses on if you don't want to go blind, like I just did. They block out 98.5 percent of the sun's harmful UV rays."

That's when some links popped up out of the sand, mostly offering more information on Tropic Ray sunglasses—different styles and prescription options.

"Wait a minute." Ashley scratched her head. "So that's what blinded you? Looking at the sun? That's not what your story is about."

"It's not? Huh… Well, I may be a bit lost, but I didn't think I was *that* far off."

Ashley looked at her brother. This Saul of Tarsus wasn't the same one they remembered from the Bible.

"No, look, sir." By this time Austin was pointing to the URL box, which read *www.paulsjourneys.net,* and to a button that said *Click Here for the Bible Story.*

But Ashley couldn't believe what they read when they did.

"'As he neared Damascus on his journey,'" Austin read from a pop-up screen, "'he looked up into the sky and was blinded by the sun.'"

"That's not how it happened!" Ashley couldn't believe someone had been messing with the Bible story that way. "What happened to the voice? What happened to Jesus telling Saul to stop persecuting him and to go into the city? Where's the rest of the story?"

But the story on this Web site had skipped all those details. And *this* Saul of Tarsus stared at her with an odd, empty expression as he rubbed his chin.

"It's like a dream…" he whispered, seeming to look off into the distance. "I remember only parts."

"It's the same as when Marco Polo's site was changed!" Austin jumped into action. "We have to reteach you what really happened."

We do? Ashley looked around nervously. She hadn't forgotten about being deleted. And she hadn't forgotten it could happen again.

CHAPTER 21

Reprogramming Saul And...

"You've got it!" After a few minutes Austin smiled at Saul of Tarsus and patted him on the back. And for the first time, the Web-site character even smiled back.

"I just needed a little reminder, that's all." Saul—soon to be renamed Paul—shrugged. His foggy expression was gone. "Thanks for helping me remember what happened in the book of Acts. Name me a verse, and I'll recite it for you."

"Acts chapter nine, verse eighteen," Mr. Webster called out a random passage.

" 'Immediately, something like scales fell from Saul's eyes, and he could see again.' " Still-blind Saul was smiling the entire time he recited the words. " 'He got up and was baptized.' "

"How about Acts nine, verse twenty-two," said Ashley.

Saul didn't skip a beat.

" 'Saul grew more and more powerful and baffled the Jews living in Damascus by proving that Jesus is the Christ.' "

"How about forty-five thousand fettuccine?" yelled someone else.

They all turned around to see a green-suited pasta worker from *www.Rigatelli-Pasta.com,* his arms spread wide.

"Ring the bell, Antonio!"

"Wait!" Austin had no idea how this was happening. "You're not supposed to be here. You can't cross over from another Web site. That doesn't happen."

The guy shrugged.

"What can I tell you? One second I was minding my own business, ringing up a sale back at the site. And the next second, *pop-pop!* I'm here. I don't explain things. I just do pasta."

"Hold it." Austin held up his hand. "You said 'pop-pop.' What's that supposed to mean?"

"Pop-pop's a sound effect. That's what it sounded like when I was pulled to this site. And I tell you what, it's not much to write home about. I'm liking the pasta kitchen a lot more than this."

That was just the beginning. Now quick *pop-pop-pops* were coming from all directions.

Everyone hunkered down.

"Can somebody tell me what's going on?" Saul asked. His vision wouldn't come back till later in his story. "What's all the popping?"

Austin wasn't quite sure how to explain what had just

appeared at the far side of the Web page. But he figured now would be a good time to run.

"Jump!" Mr. Webster tried to herd everyone off to the side before the Polo expedition camels trampled them. They tumbled into a shallow ditch next to the road to Damascus.

"Sorry!" Marco called down to them from the back of one of the beasts. "These things don't handle very well."

"You should see him try to park!" yelled Uncle Matteo, waving his hands from the back of his own camel. Niccolo Polo wasn't having any better luck, though he might have earned a few extra points in a rodeo competition.

While the Polos were doing their best to bring their camels under control, the Machu Picchu T-shirt vendor popped up by the side of the road, his wares draped over both arms. He looked down at Austin and the others in the ditch and grinned.

"Looks like you folks could use some souvenirs. Regular price? Five dollars. But for you…"

"Why am I not surprised?" Austin sat up for a better look. By that time old URL had taken up a spot a few yards away in his rocking chair and was watching the whole crazy parade. All he needed was a glass of lemonade and a little flag to wave. Two guides from the Lost Sea Cave Web site had even shown up with flashlights.

And, of course, it had to happen: Cindy had also joined

them by now, bringing hundreds of her cute, adoptable critters from *www.LostKitty.com* along for the ride. The furry bundles streamed across the road, mewing and climbing all over everyone in sight.

Meanwhile the virtual Lewis and Clark expedition was pushing and pulling its canoes across the road, grunting to heave-hos and looking mighty perplexed.

"Check your map again, Meriwether!" Clark was not a happy camper. "I'm positive there's supposed to be a river here someplace."

There wasn't, of course.

Bump, bump, bump! Amelia Earhart's plane landed from its low approach right onto the desert flats not far from the road. As the plane taxied closer, Fred Noonan popped out the side window and leaned his head out.

"Hey, kids!" He looked straight at Austin and Ashley. "Remember that *NCCC-dot-org* that was watching you?"

Austin and Ashley shielded their faces as the plane kicked up the dust, and Mr. Noonan pointed over their shoulders.

"Well, there's your man!"

CHAPTER 22

Zoot!

This would have been a great time to find a nice link to take them home. Or maybe a button that said Escape, and they would. But none of that happened, and Ashley gulped when she saw Mr. Z headed their way, briefcase in hand as he made entries in a new-looking handheld computer.

"That's Mr. Z," she croaked, but the whisper didn't quite graduate from her throat.

Austin slipped his laptop behind his back and passed it to Ashley for safekeeping.

Just in case.

"Hey, there!" The substitute-teacher-turned-bad-guy smiled as he stepped around the guy selling Lost City T-shirts. One by one the Web characters were disappearing again.

Zoot! Amelia Earhart and Fred Noonan disappeared first.

Zoot-zoot. There went Marco Polo and his camels, with a quick wave good-bye.

Mr. Z paused to look up from his handheld computer.

"I am so glad I caught up with you folks."

I'll bet you are, Ashley thought as she glanced at her brother, who had squared his jaw and clenched his fists. Austin seemed ready for anything as Mr. Z introduced himself to their parents as a former substitute teacher from back home. Yeah, he was that—and a lot more. Now would be a great time to explain the *whole* story to their parents.

But Mr. Z beat them to it. "You folks certainly deserve an explanation," he said, putting on a friendly face and rubbing his hands together. "You're probably wondering how I found you in here."

"Well…" Austin's dad looked totally confused. Hard not to, with all they had been through. The rest of the digital characters kept zooting out of there one at a time, leaving only the dusty landscape. Even the apostle Paul disappeared without a word.

"It's a long story, actually." This guy was good; Ashley had to grant him that. When he wanted to, he could pour on the charm thick. For a moment even Ashley wondered if this was really the same person who had tried so hard to steal Austin's camera and laptop and had done so much to change the Internet—and had probably even tried to delete them.

"Well, we've actually been running into a few problems." Mr. Webster cleared his throat. "And I don't mean all these characters that just piled up here."

"Ah, so we had a little glitch, eh?" Mr. Z looked around. "Glad I could help take care of it."

"Right. But for a while it seemed like somebody was... well...after us."

"Don't I know it!" Mr. Z shook his head as if he knew exactly what they'd been going through. "I was running into some of the same thing myself. Very irritating. Bad programming here and there sometimes makes it hard to get around on the Web."

Bad programming! Hardly!

"The only bad programming is what you and Ms. Blankenskrean do!" Austin blurted out.

Their mother gasped. "Austin! I'm sure Mr. Zawistokowski was only trying to help us. He was your *teacher,* remember. You shouldn't—"

"But, Mom, you don't understand! He—"

"Austin!" snapped his father. "That's enough."

"That's all right." Mr. Z put up his hand. "The boy has a point, and I actually do have a major apology to make. To all four of you."

"You do?" Austin backed off for a moment as they waited for Mr. Z to explain.

Mr. Z studied the dusty ground for a second before looking up again.

"I do. And I honestly was only trying to help locate you

folks. But I'm afraid that in the process, my program may have malfunctioned. So instead of rescuing you the way I'd hoped, your files were misplaced for a short time. It was a terrible mistake."

"So *you* were the one who put us in the trash?" their dad asked.

"And I am so sorry about that. I just want you to know I did everything in my power to make things right. But listen, I'd like to make it up to you. Offer you a way out, back to Normal."

Their mom smiled, and Ashley felt like shouting, *No! It's a trick!*

"That's very kind of you, Mr. Zawisto—"

"Please." He held up his hand like a performer directing the audience to stop clapping. "Call me Mr. Z. The kids all do, right, Abby?"

"Ashley." Now Ashley was ready to be sick. This had to be a trick. "And—"

"No, it's me who's sorry. I was trying to follow you from the Outside, but you were hopping from site to site so fast I couldn't keep up. Finally I decided to come in person. Frankly, I was worried about your safety."

"That's real decent of you, Mr. Z." Like their mom, their dad had been taken in by the con man. "Real decent. But we have another girl we need to return to at a campground.

Evelyne's little sister. So we really need to get back to someplace a little closer to that than Normal."

"Ah yes…Jessica. I can arrange for that. Lost Lake Resort, isn't it?"

"Wow. For a teacher, you sure do your homework."

Mr. Z shrugged and held up his hands. "That's what I do. In fact…"

To everyone's surprise, the kitty stampede suddenly circled around again, only this time no one had time to move out of the way.

Mee-OWWW! Thousands of fur balls hit at the same time, knocking Ashley and the others off their feet. She did her best to keep Austin's laptop from hitting the ground, but it slipped out of her grip. And each time she tried to get up, another wave of kitties hit from the opposite direction. She rolled a few times and got to her knees.

"Sorry!" The cat woman tried to herd her animals as they thundered through the Web site. Well, if kittens could thunder.

The weird thing was, these cats were stampeding around almost as if they were being steered with a remote control. Wave after wave of them.

And then as quickly as they'd come, they were gone. *Zoot!* Mr. Z finished keying in something on his handheld, slipped it into his pocket, and helped Ashley's parents to their feet.

"Well, that's taken care of," he told them. "I don't think

we're going to have any more use for—I mean, well, they're gone."

But Ashley was hardly listening. She was combing the ground in a panic. *Where is it?* Austin joined her when he realized what had happened. They couldn't lose his computer now!

"Looking for this?" Mr. Z held Austin's laptop out to her with a smile. Ashley's jaw must have hit the ground. *Where did he... How did he...*

"Uh, yeah." Well, that didn't sound very intelligent. But it was the only thing she could manage. Maybe she *had* been wrong about Mr. Z.

"I thought it belonged to you two." He handed it over. "Wouldn't want you to lose it here inside the Internet."

Austin mumbled a "thanks" as he took it back and slipped it under his arm. Her brother was going to have to get a case for that old thing, though it really didn't look as scratched up as it could have, considering. Well, at least he took good care of it—most of the time.

"And now"—Mr. Z patted his briefcase and pointed toward a hill—"I'll escort you all to your link."

Seemed Like a Nice Man

"Did you make the switch?" Mattie Blankenskrean leaned in as Mr. Z set his briefcase up on the desk with a proud smile.

"Of course I did. With my humble act, they didn't suspect a thing. Doing that was better than deleting them, don't you think?"

He took his time snapping the briefcase open. They had waited this long to finally grab this prize. Mattie could wait a few more moments.

"So it was the cats?" she asked.

"I steered them in circles so they knocked the Websters off their feet, just the way we'd planned."

"And who had the laptop, the boy or the girl?"

"The girl. I saw Austin hand it to her as soon as I showed up."

"Excellent. And she—"

"She dropped it, fortunately. Made the switch that much

easier. When everything was over, I simply handed her the replacement. You should have seen her face."

He laughed as Mattie reached for the briefcase, but he blocked her hand. He liked the way he felt now—in charge.

"But what would you have done if she hadn't dropped it?" she asked.

"I had a backup plan." He smiled. "But it doesn't matter. We have the computer now. And you don't have to worry about the Websters returning to the Internet to interfere with anything ever again. That digital camera of theirs seems to work only with Austin's old computer. Must be an odd glitch in the hard drive."

Of course Mr. Z was playing this for all it was worth. But at last he had to open the case and pull out the scratched old laptop that had caused them so much grief. With a little bow, he served it up like a waiter at a fancy restaurant.

And he waited.

Actually, the computer seemed a bit lighter than he had expected. Probably nothing. And he didn't notice the square hole in its side until he looked more closely. By that time Mattie had already grabbed it.

"I suppose you're going to tell me you didn't realize it didn't have the memory pack when you took it," she growled.

His mouth went dry, and he tried to spit out an answer.

"Good job," she managed as she threw the laptop across

the room. It shattered against the far wall. "You brought home the useless case. The kids still have the *brains* of the machine!"

"Well I thought he seemed like a very nice man." Ashley's mom hurried across the parking lot from the Lost Lake Resort store. Hopefully Jessi would still be waiting for them back at the minivan. After all, if the clock in the store was right, they'd been gone less than two hours.

Ashley's head was still spinning as she tried to sort things out. She didn't dare tell anyone yet about the wiggly ball of fur that had followed her back to the resort.

"That's just it, Mom," Austin told them. "He's not. He was just putting on a show."

"You shouldn't say things like that about your teacher." Their dad led the way back to the van and tent trailer. "He went out of his way to help us."

"But—" Austin started to say something else and then must have changed his mind.

How could Austin still be so sure Mr. Z was up to no good? Ashley's eyes fell on her brother's computer as they walked.

Hadn't the cover been much more scratched up than that before? And when he opened it, it started right up, just like that.

With what battery?

Well, maybe it had somehow gotten recharged on their last hyperlink here. Ashley didn't really know what was possible. Still, she didn't understand why Austin grinned as he pulled his laptop's memory pack from his pocket.

"And now that we're back," their mom broke in, "I want you to make good on your promise to do fun outdoor things this vacation, not walk around with your nose stuck in that computer."

Austin plugged his memory pack into the side of the laptop before he shut it down and folded it up.

"I know, Mom," he said with a laugh. "Active stuff. I promise."

The HyperLinkz Guide to Safe Surfing

Hey, bloggers and blogettes! Austin T. Webster here, having the time of my life at the Lost Lake Resort. Wish you were here and all that...

Ashley: Blogette is not a word, Austin.

Austin: Maybe not, but it fits into the story pretty well.

Ashley: Okay, but I have a question. Do you need a computer to write a blog?

Austin: Officially, yes. A blog is a Web log somebody keeps. But that doesn't mean you can't write a diary or the story of your life, even if you don't post it up on the Web for the whole world to see. In fact, that's probably a great idea. An unplugged blog—an unblog.

Ashley: All right, then, our unblog is going to tell all about the real Marco Polo, Amelia Earhart, and other lost people and things. First Marco Polo...

Austin: He wrote a book, called *The Travels of Marco Polo,* about traveling to China from Italy starting in the year 1271, when he was seventeen. He went exploring with his dad and uncle. That's where we got the true story of the one hundred missionaries who were invited to China—but never showed up!

Ashley: Problem was, Marco's adventures seemed so fantastic that some people back then didn't believe him. In fact, some people today don't. Austin and I can relate.

Austin: No kidding! A priest actually asked Marco Polo, who was on his deathbed, if he wanted to take it all back. You know, admit he'd been lying? Marco said, "I do not tell half of what I saw because no one would have believed me."

Ashley: True or not, there is a whole lot of stuff on the Web about Marco. There are lots of sites you can check out.

Austin: Just don't try to visit the one we went to in the story. Remember, most of the Web addresses in the story are made up.

Ashley: Right. So try *http://cybersleuth-kids.com/sleuth/ History/Explorers/Marco_Polo/index.htm*. (That's without a period at the end and an underscore between Marco and Polo.)

Austin: There's also a cool little Q&A by a missionary to Italy who answers the all-important question: Did Marco Polo bring back spaghetti to Italy from China? Go to *http://home .snu.edu/~hculbert/pasta5.htm* for that.

Ashley: You always manage to bring in a little bit of food trivia, don't you?

Austin: As long as it's not about tofu.

Ashley: Okay, Austin. You already took a shot at tofu in this story, but lots of people really like it, especially in countries like Japan and China. And it's really good for you.

Austin: I'll always like pasta better. Did you know I found a long list of all kinds of pasta? Like mezzi bombardoni and tortiglioni and a bunch of others you might not be able to pronounce. Try *www.sciencedaily.com/encyclopedia/pasta.*

Ashley: Impressive. But before we run out of time, we'd better tell people about a few other real sites that link back to our story. Like *www.ameliaearhartmuseum.org,* which will tell you all about Amelia Earhart. She was one of the early great women aviators. The sad part is that she really was lost at sea, in the middle of the Pacific, trying to become the first woman to fly around the world.

Austin: Another site you can visit is *www.thelostsea.com,* which is about America's largest underground lake, near beautiful Sweetwater, Tennessee. It's a very cool place in more ways than one.

Ashley: And one more thing: Our story was all about being lost. But how about if we end up by talking about being *found* for a change?

Austin: Hmm… You mean like when we found Aunt Jessi back at the camp? Or your cyberkitty? Or when Saul of Tarsus found—

Ashley: Whoa! You're going to give the best part away.

Better to check out Acts chapter nine in the Bible to find out what in the world my brother is talking about.

Austin: Can I say it's the ultimate road unblog—all about what Saul found on his way to Damascus?

Ashley: You just did!

See ya,

Austin and Ashley

P.S. to parents: The Internet can be a lot of fun, but please make sure your child is surfing safely. That means being there for them. Know what they're accessing. And consider using a good filtering service or software; it can help you sidestep some nasty surprises. While we can't tell you which filter is best for your family's needs, you might begin by checking out a great site called *www.filterreview.com*. It will give you many of the options so you can make a wise decision.

Please visit the author's Web site at *www.RobertElmerBooks.com* to learn more about other books he's written or to schedule him to speak to your school or home-school group.